Anouk Ricard

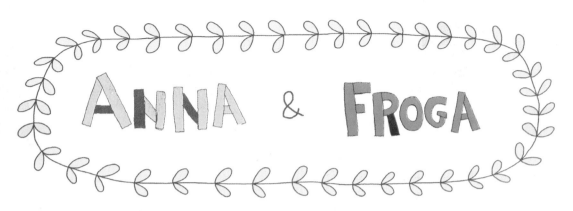

ANNA & FROGA

Thrills, spills, and gooseberries

PITCH 'N WIN

100% OF WINNERS
WIN PRIZES!

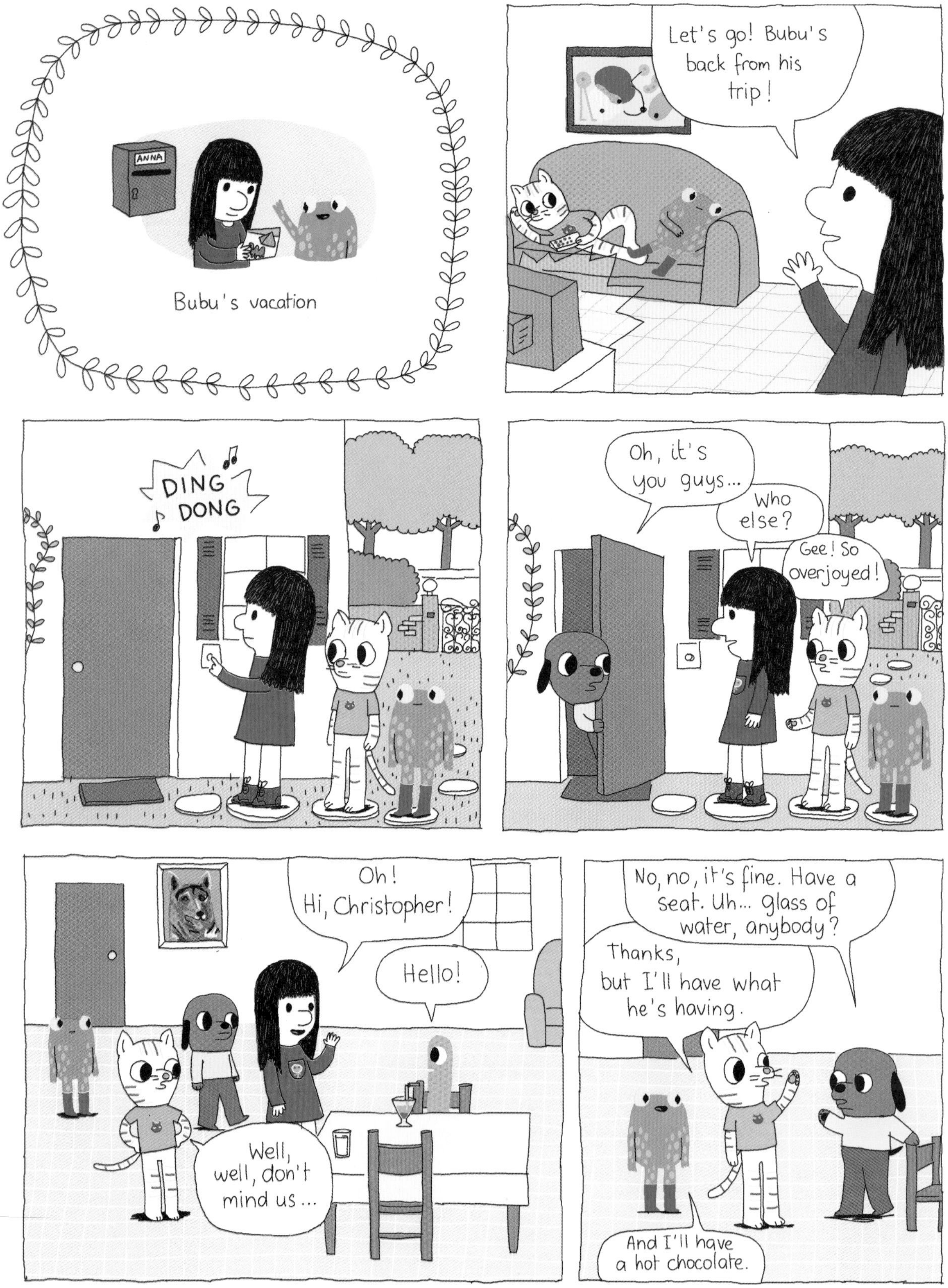
ANNA
Bubu's vacation
Let's go! Bubu's back from his trip!
DING DONG
Oh, it's you guys...
Who else?
Gee! So overjoyed!
Oh! Hi, Christopher!
Hello!
Well, well, don't mind us...
No, no, it's fine. Have a seat. Uh... glass of water, anybody?
Thanks, but I'll have what he's having.
And I'll have a hot chocolate.

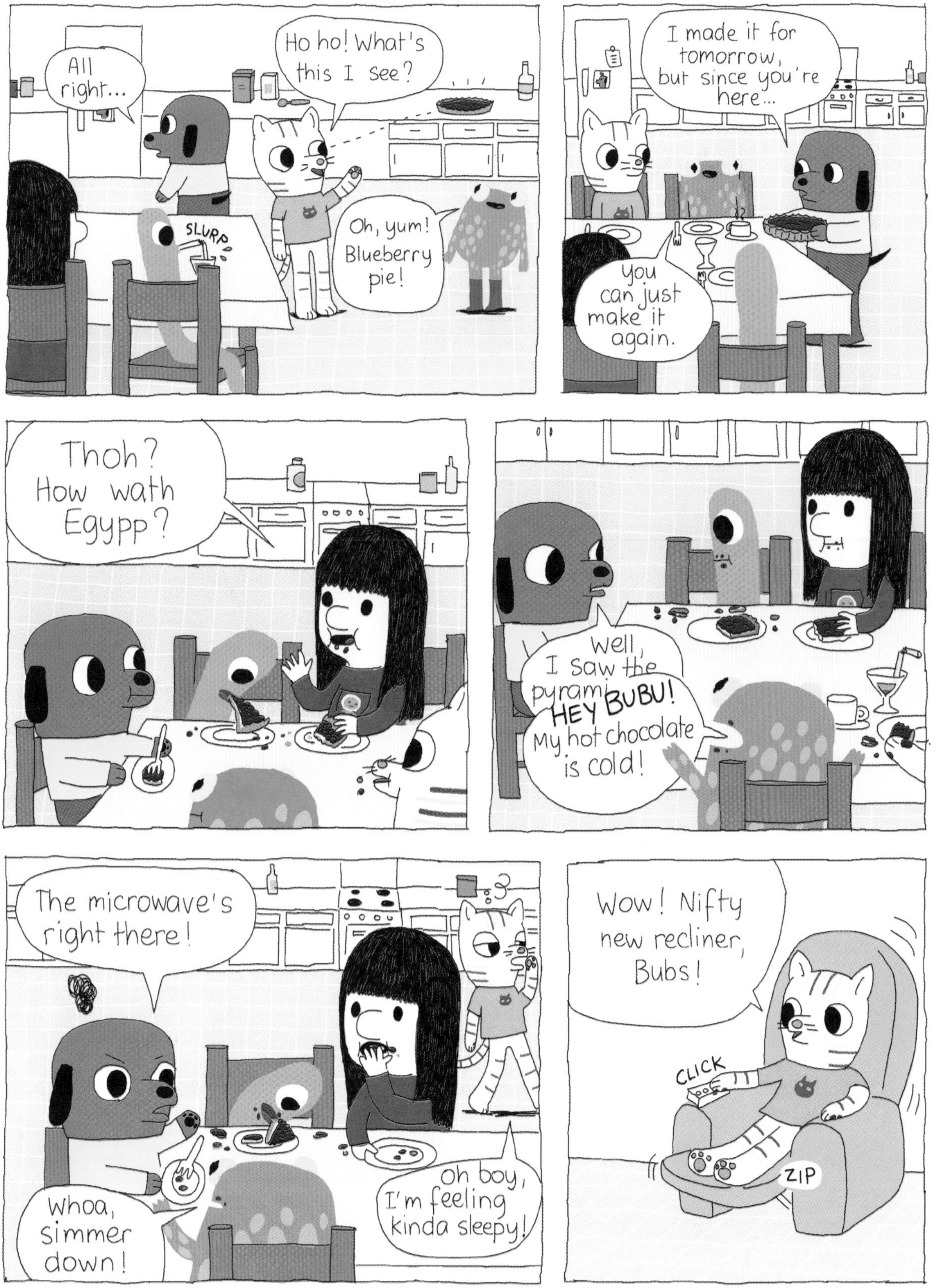
All right...
Ho ho! What's this I see?
SLURP
Oh, yum! Blueberry pie!
I made it for tomorrow, but since you're here...
You can just make it again.
Thoh? How wath Egypp?
Well, I saw the pyrami
HEY BUBU! My hot chocolate is cold!
The microwave's right there!
Whoa, simmer down!
Oh boy, I'm feeling kinda sleepy!
Wow! Nifty new recliner, Bubs!
CLICK
ZIP

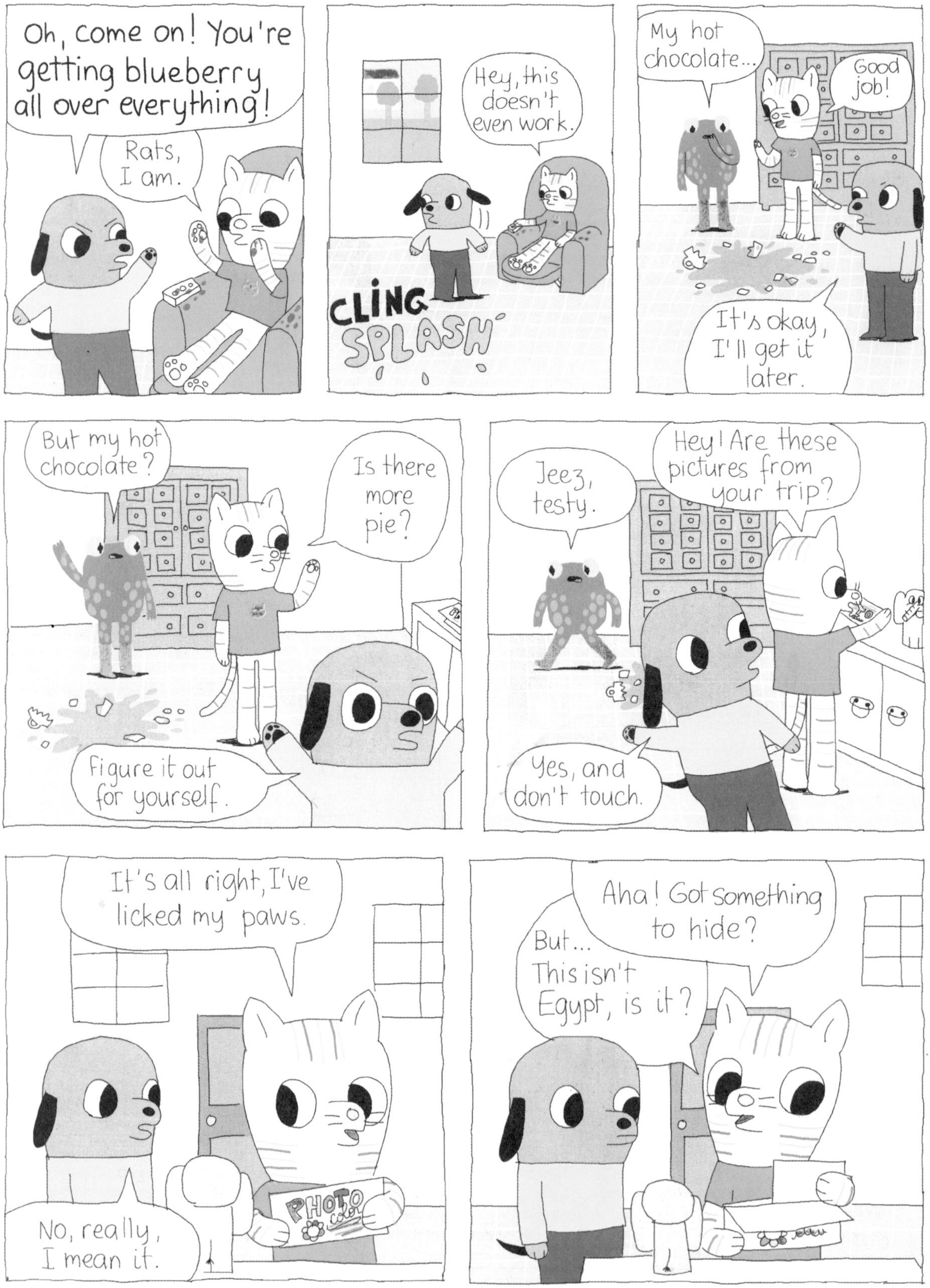
Oh, come on! You're getting blueberry all over everything!
Rats, I am.
Hey, this doesn't even work.
CLING
SPLASH
My hot chocolate...
Good job!
It's okay, I'll get it later.
But my hot chocolate?
Is there more pie?
Figure it out for yourself.
Jeez, testy.
Hey! Are these pictures from your trip?
Yes, and don't touch.
It's all right, I've licked my paws.
No, really, I mean it.
PHOTO color
Aha! Got something to hide?
But... This isn't Egypt, is it?

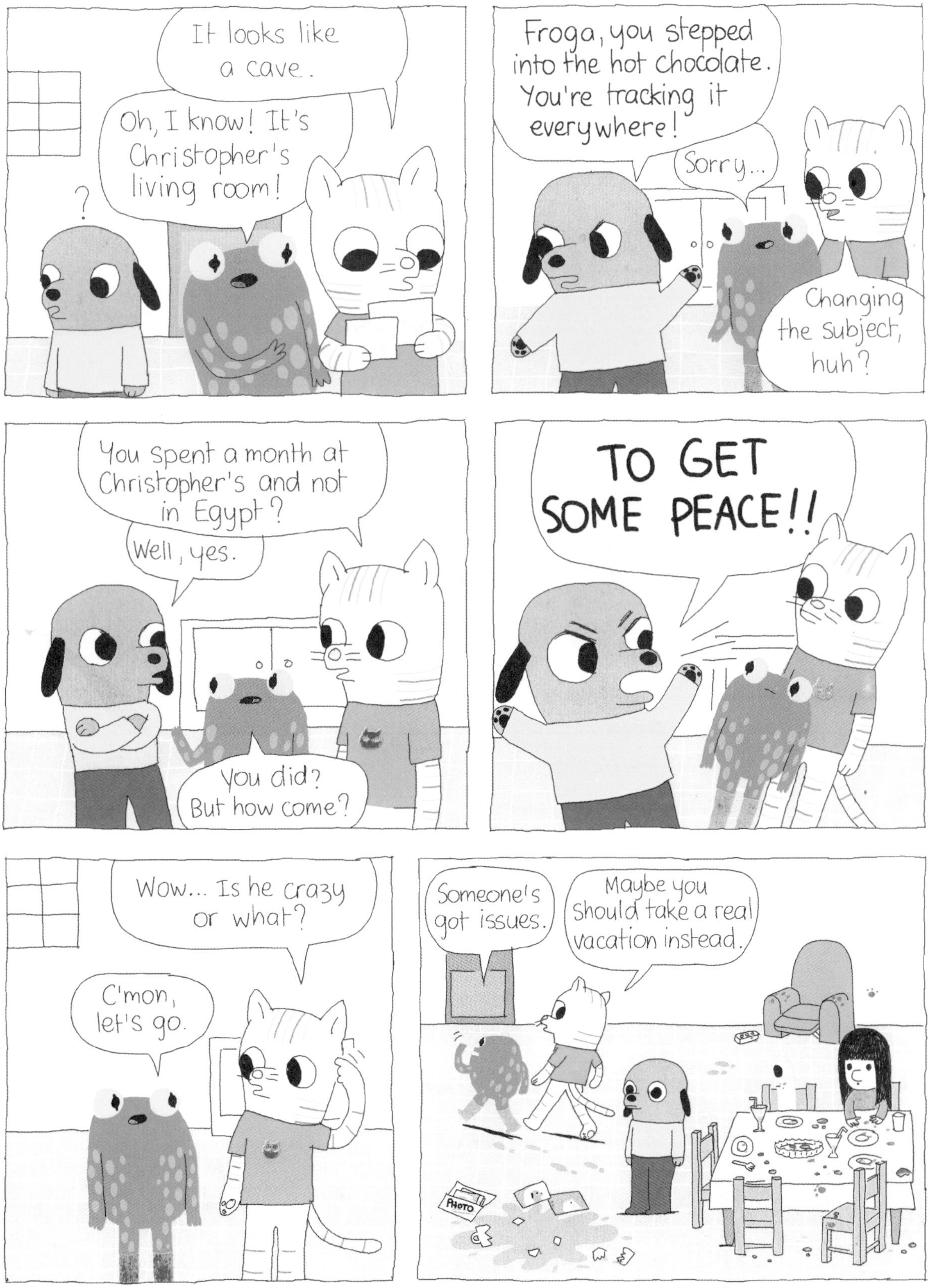
It looks like a cave.
Oh, I know! It's Christopher's living room!
?
Froga, you stepped into the hot chocolate. You're tracking it everywhere!
Sorry...
Changing the subject, huh?
You spent a month at Christopher's and not in Egypt?
Well, yes.
You did? But how come?
TO GET SOME PEACE!!
Wow... Is he crazy or what?
C'mon, let's go.
Someone's got issues.
Maybe you should take a real vacation instead.
PHOTO

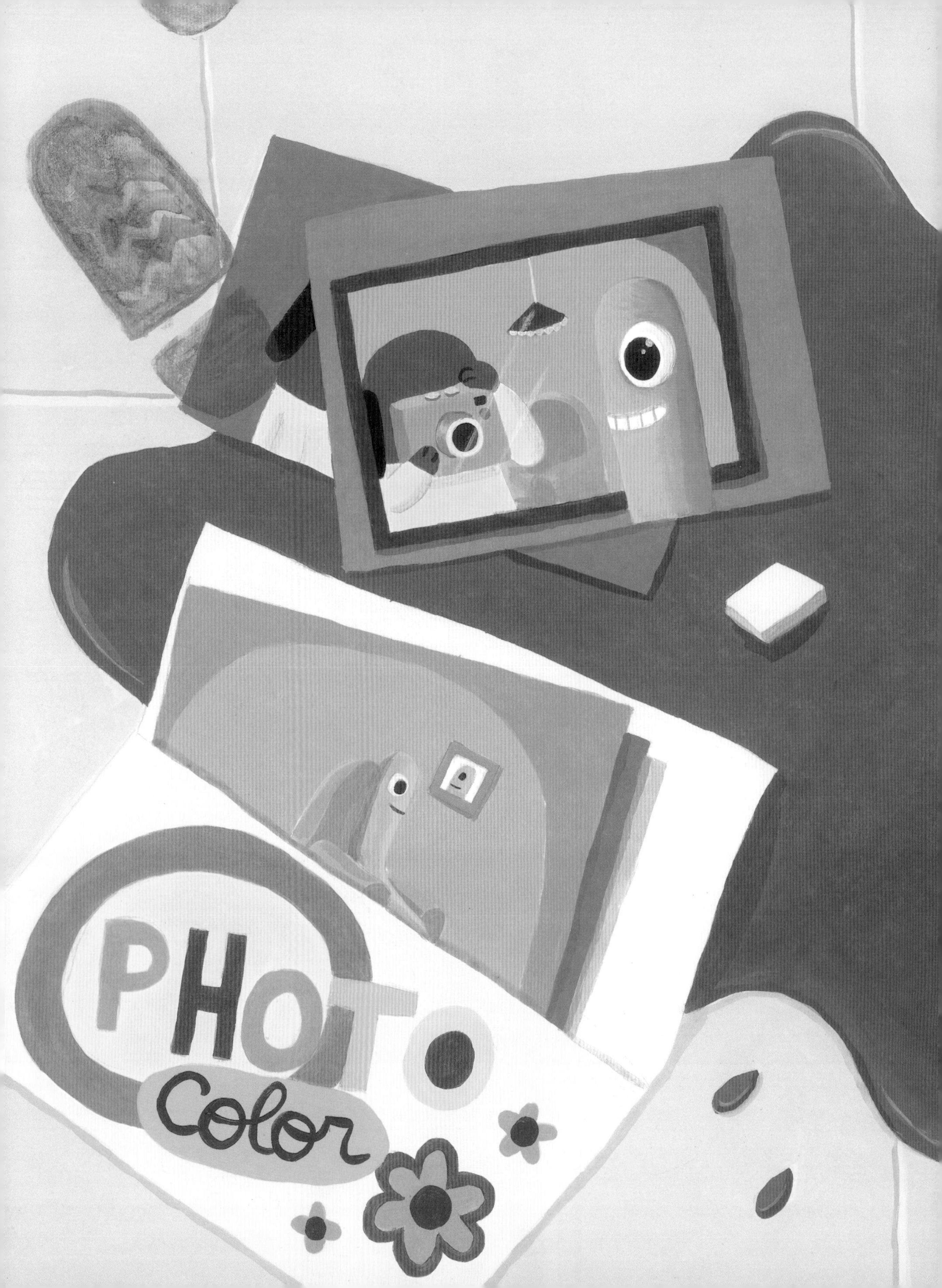
PHOTO
Color

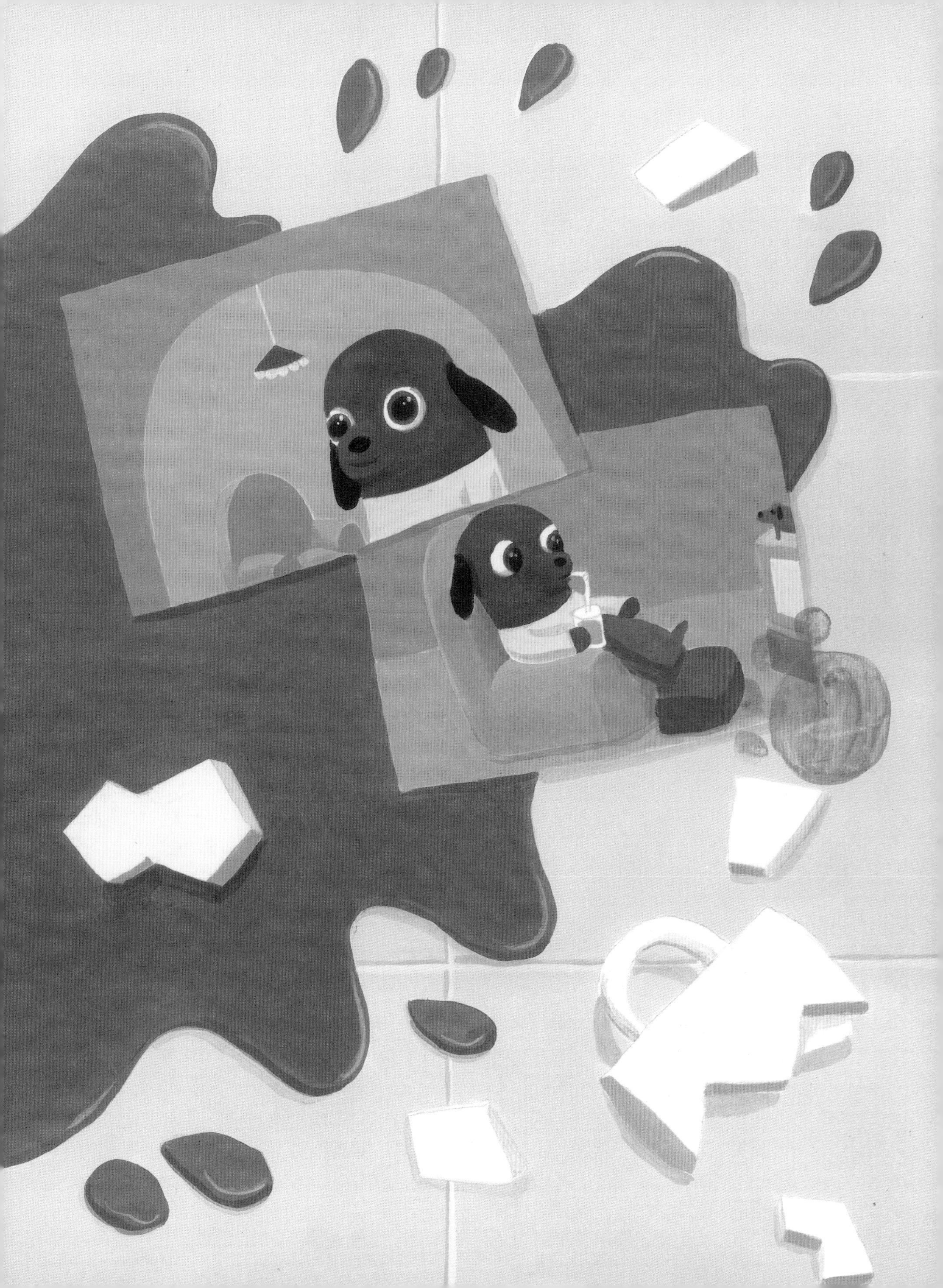

Frogo's garden

The rose

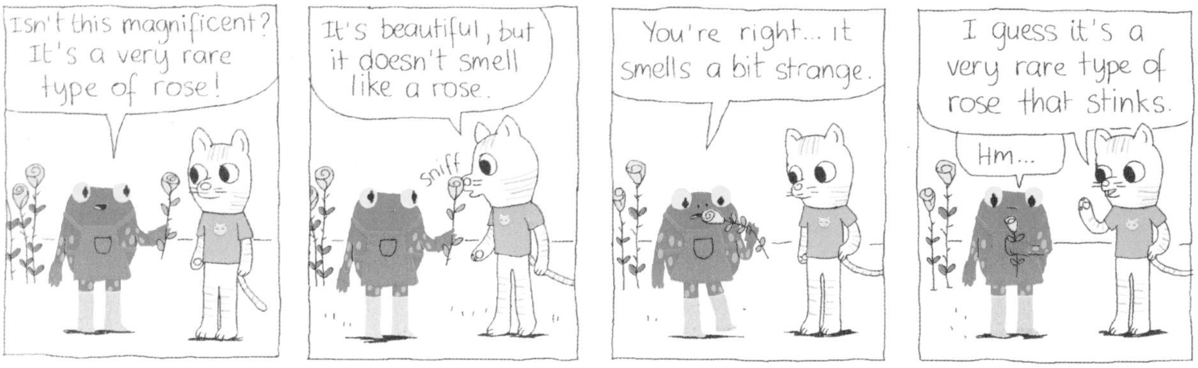
Isn't this magnificent? It's a very rare type of rose!
It's beautiful, but it doesn't smell like a rose.
sniff
You're right... it smells a bit strange.
I guess it's a very rare type of rose that stinks.
Hm...

Begonias, etc.

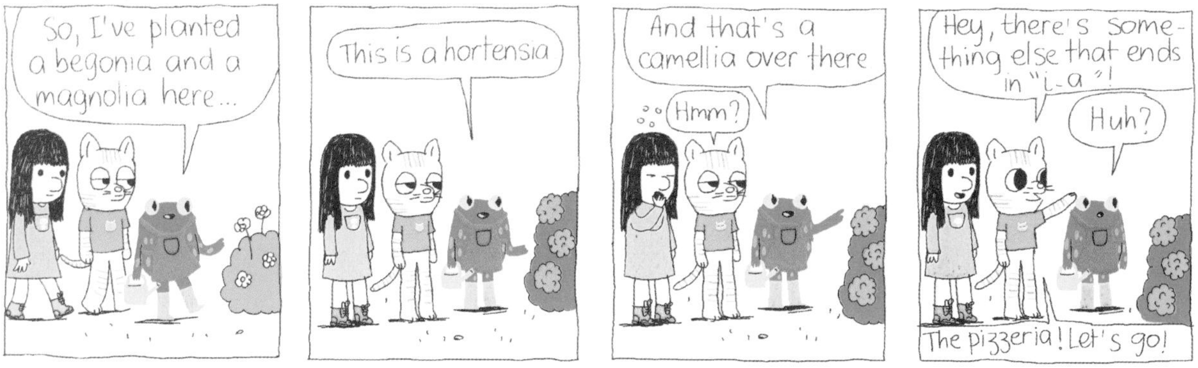
So, I've planted a begonia and a magnolia here...
This is a hortensia
And that's a camellia over there
Hmm?
Hey, there's something else that ends in "i-a"!
Huh?
The pizzeria! Let's go!

The snail

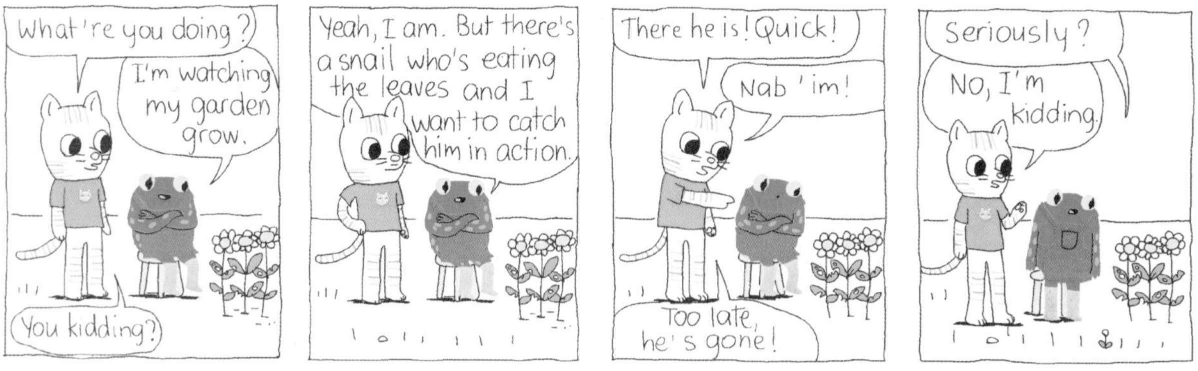
What're you doing?
I'm watching my garden grow.
You kidding?
Yeah, I am. But there's a snail who's eating the leaves and I want to catch him in action.
There he is! Quick!
Nab 'im!
Too late, he's gone!
Seriously?
No, I'm kidding.

Apples

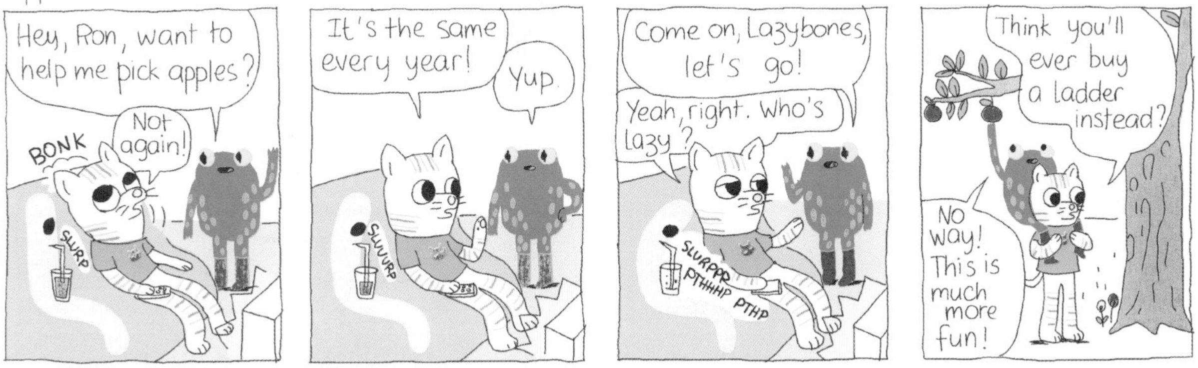
Hey, Ron, want to help me pick apples?
BONK
Not again!
SLURP
It's the same every year!
Yup.
SLUUURP
Come on, Lazybones, let's go!
Yeah, right. Who's lazy?
SLURPPP PTHHHP PTHP
Think you'll ever buy a ladder instead?
No way! This is much more fun!

The cabbage

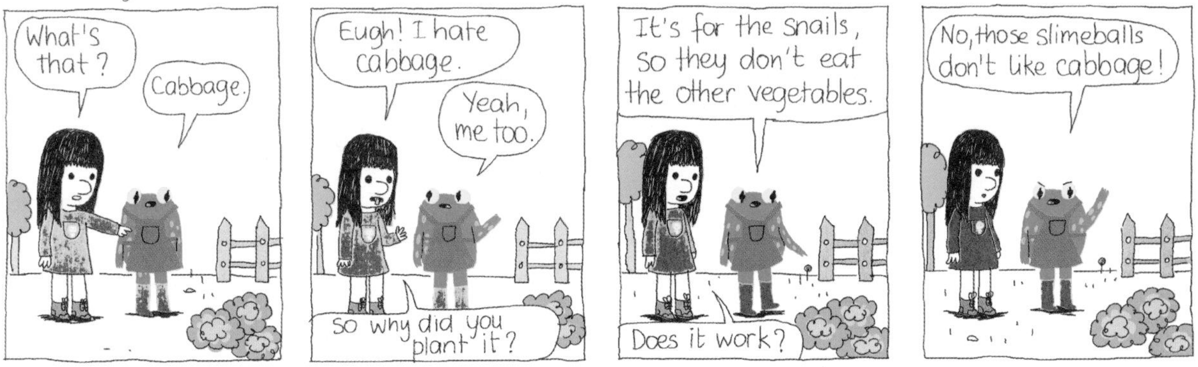
What's that?
Cabbage.
Eugh! I hate cabbage.
Yeah, me too.
So why did you plant it?
It's for the snails, so they don't eat the other vegetables.
Does it work?
No, those slimeballs don't like cabbage!

The weeds

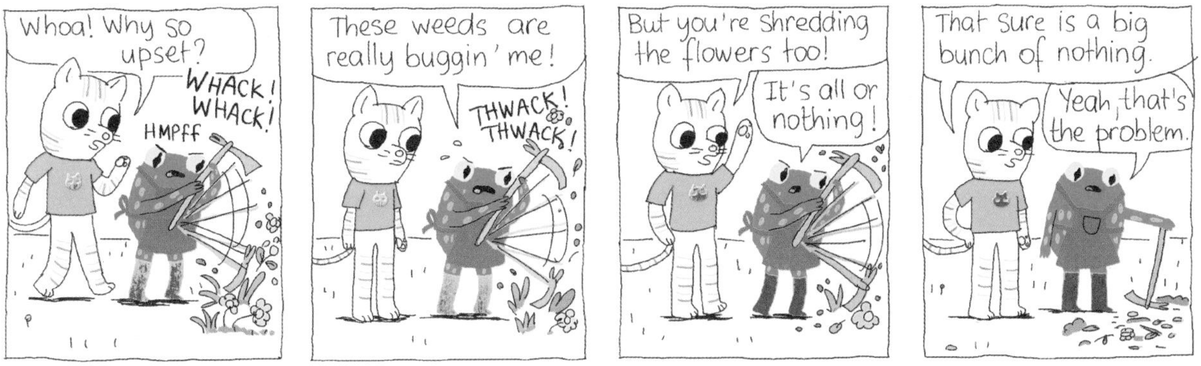
Whoa! Why so upset?
WHACK! WHACK!
HMPFF
These weeds are really buggin' me!
THWACK! THWACK!
But you're shredding the flowers too!
It's all or nothing!
That sure is a big bunch of nothing.
Yeah, that's the problem.

The strawberries

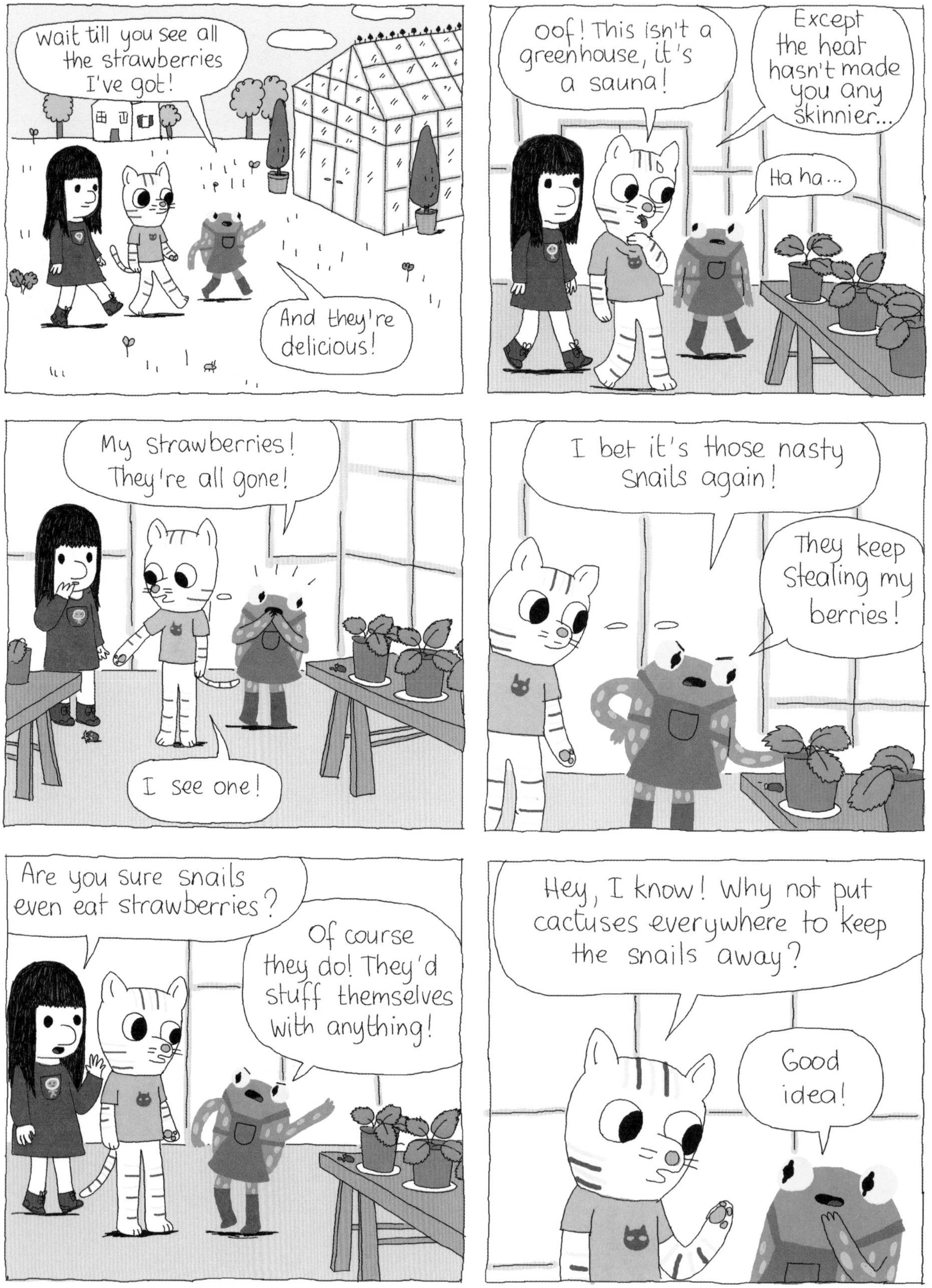

Wait till you see all the strawberries I've got!
And they're delicious!
Oof! This isn't a greenhouse, it's a sauna!
Except the heat hasn't made you any skinnier...
Ha ha...
My strawberries! They're all gone!
I see one!
I bet it's those nasty snails again!
They keep stealing my berries!
Are you sure snails even eat strawberries?
Of course they do! They'd stuff themselves with anything!
Hey, I know! Why not put cactuses everywhere to keep the snails away?
Good idea!

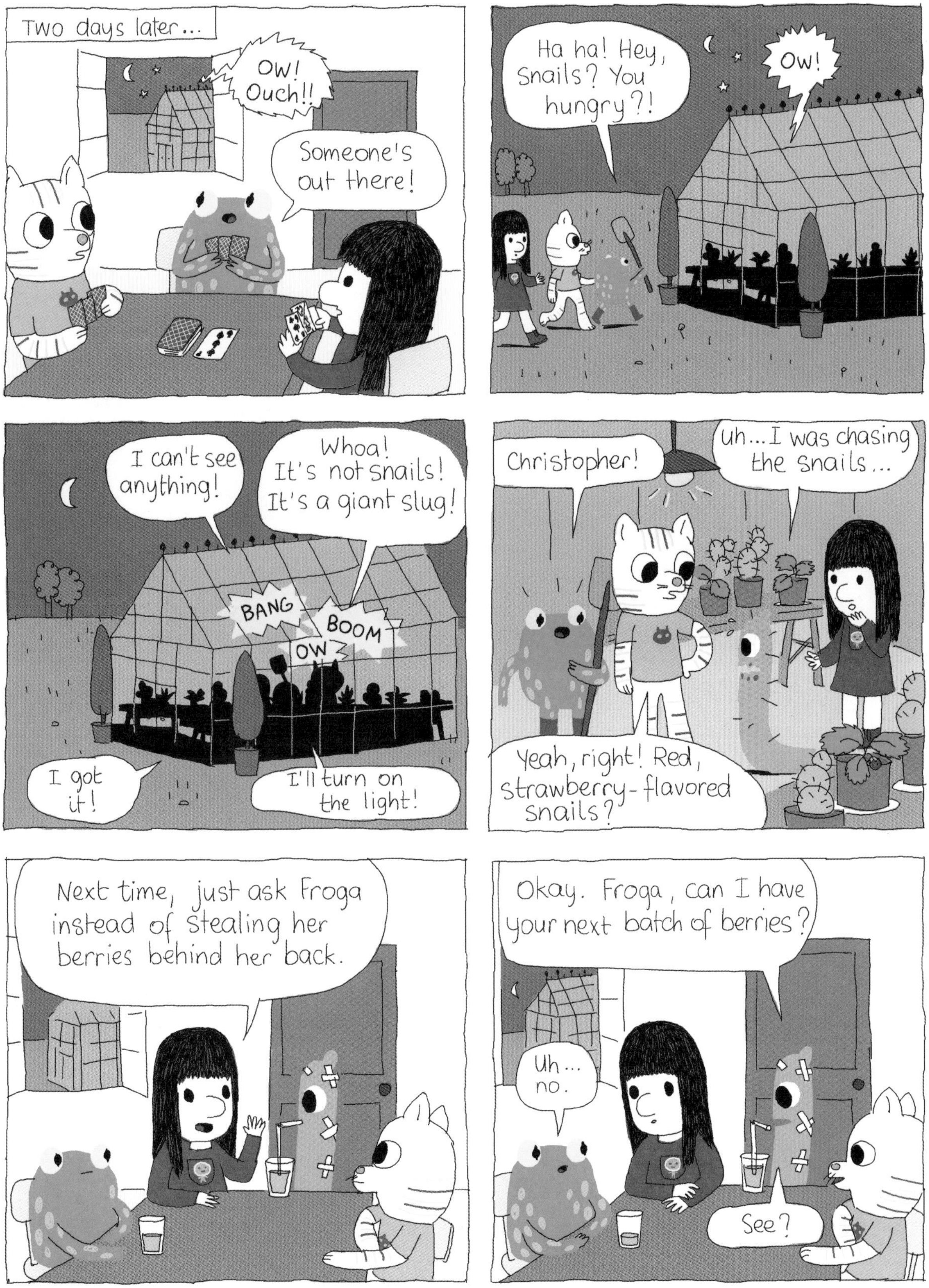
Two days later...
Ow! Ouch!!
Someone's out there!
Ha ha! Hey, Snails? You hungry?!
Ow!
I can't see anything!
Whoa! It's not snails! It's a giant slug!
BANG
BOOM
OW
I got it!
I'll turn on the light!
Christopher!
Uh... I was chasing the snails...
Yeah, right! Red, strawberry-flavored snails?
Next time, just ask Froga instead of stealing her berries behind her back.
Okay. Froga, can I have your next batch of berries?
Uh... no.
See?

- Oh, go home! All of you!

- No, I meant get out of here!

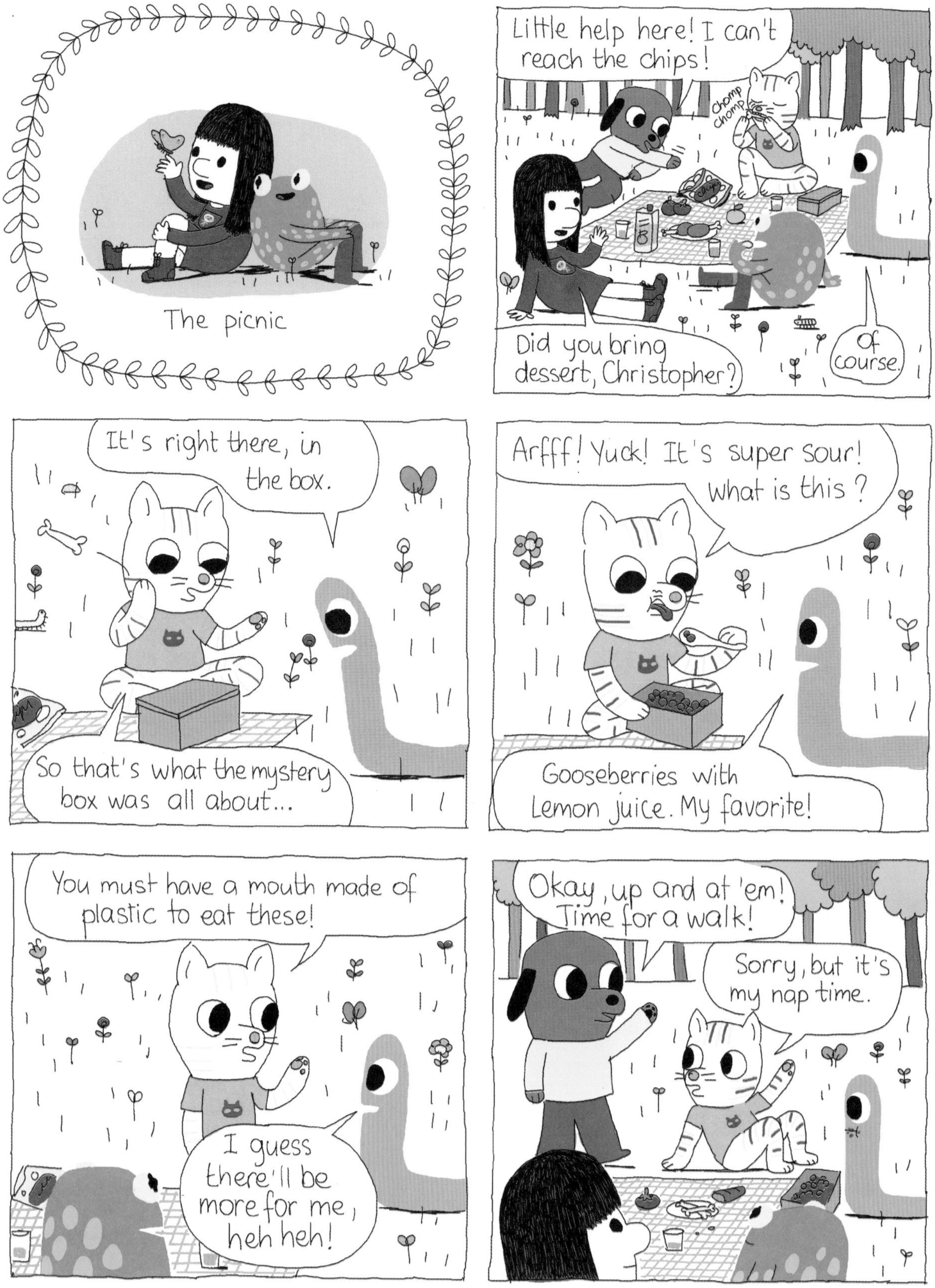
The picnic
Little help here! I can't reach the chips!
Chomp chomp
Did you bring dessert, Christopher?
Of course.
It's right there, in the box.
So that's what the mystery box was all about...
Arfff! Yuck! It's super sour! What is this?
Gooseberries with Lemon juice. My favorite!
You must have a mouth made of plastic to eat these!
I guess there'll be more for me, heh heh!
Okay, up and at 'em! Time for a walk!
Sorry, but it's my nap time.

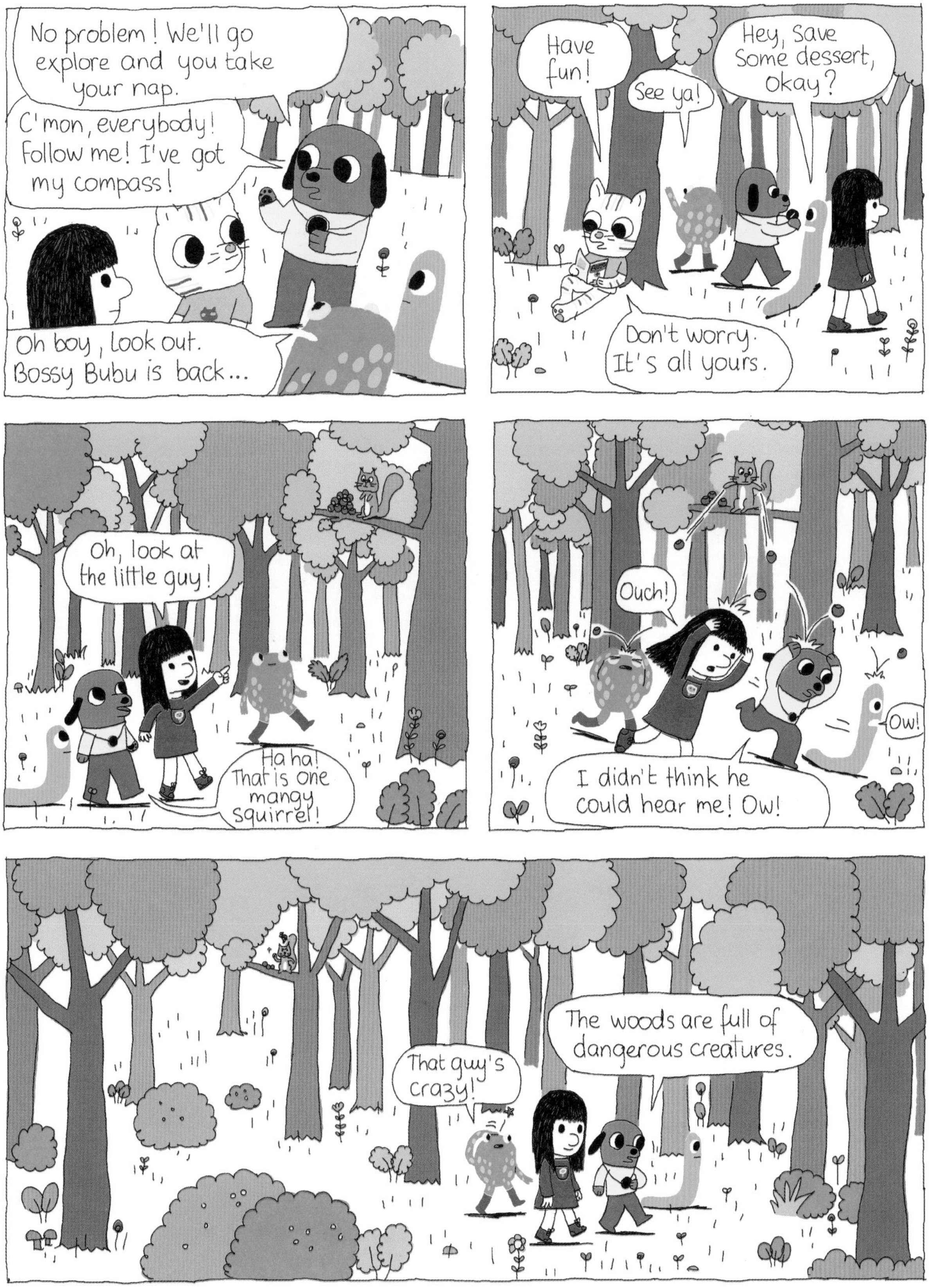
No problem! We'll go explore and you take your nap.
C'mon, everybody! Follow me! I've got my compass!
Oh boy, look out. Bossy Bubu is back...
Have fun!
See ya!
Hey, save some dessert, okay?
Don't worry. It's all yours.
Oh, look at the little guy!
Ha ha! That is one mangy squirrel!
Ouch!
Ow!
I didn't think he could hear me! Ow!
That guy's crazy!
The woods are full of dangerous creatures.

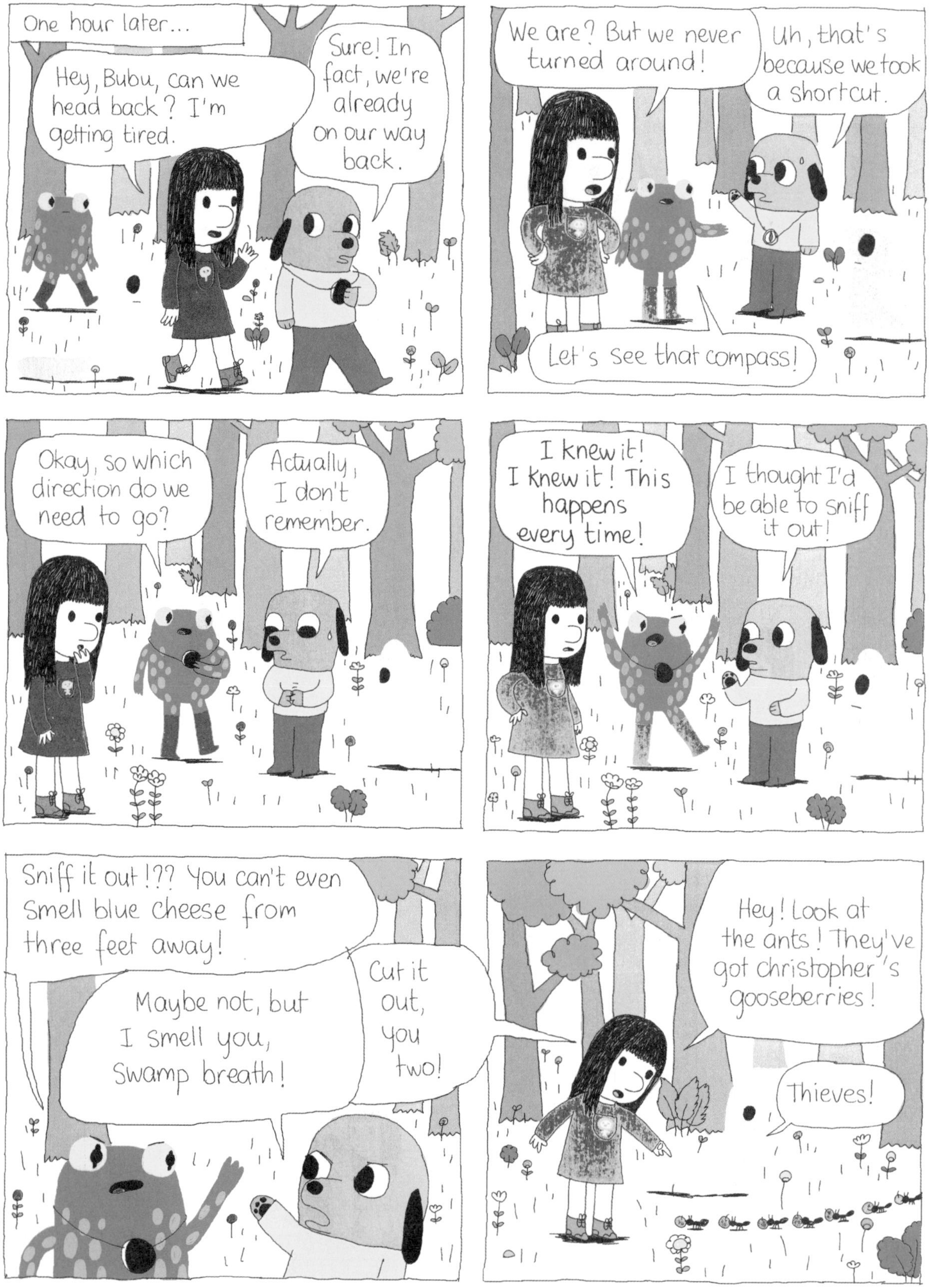
One hour later...
Hey, Bubu, can we head back? I'm getting tired.
Sure! In fact, we're already on our way back.
We are? But we never turned around!
Uh, that's because we took a shortcut.
Let's see that compass!
Okay, so which direction do we need to go?
Actually, I don't remember.
I knew it! I knew it! This happens every time!
I thought I'd be able to sniff it out!
Sniff it out!?? You can't even smell blue cheese from three feet away!
Maybe not, but I smell you, Swamp breath!
Cut it out, you two!
Hey! Look at the ants! They've got Christopher's gooseberries!
Thieves!

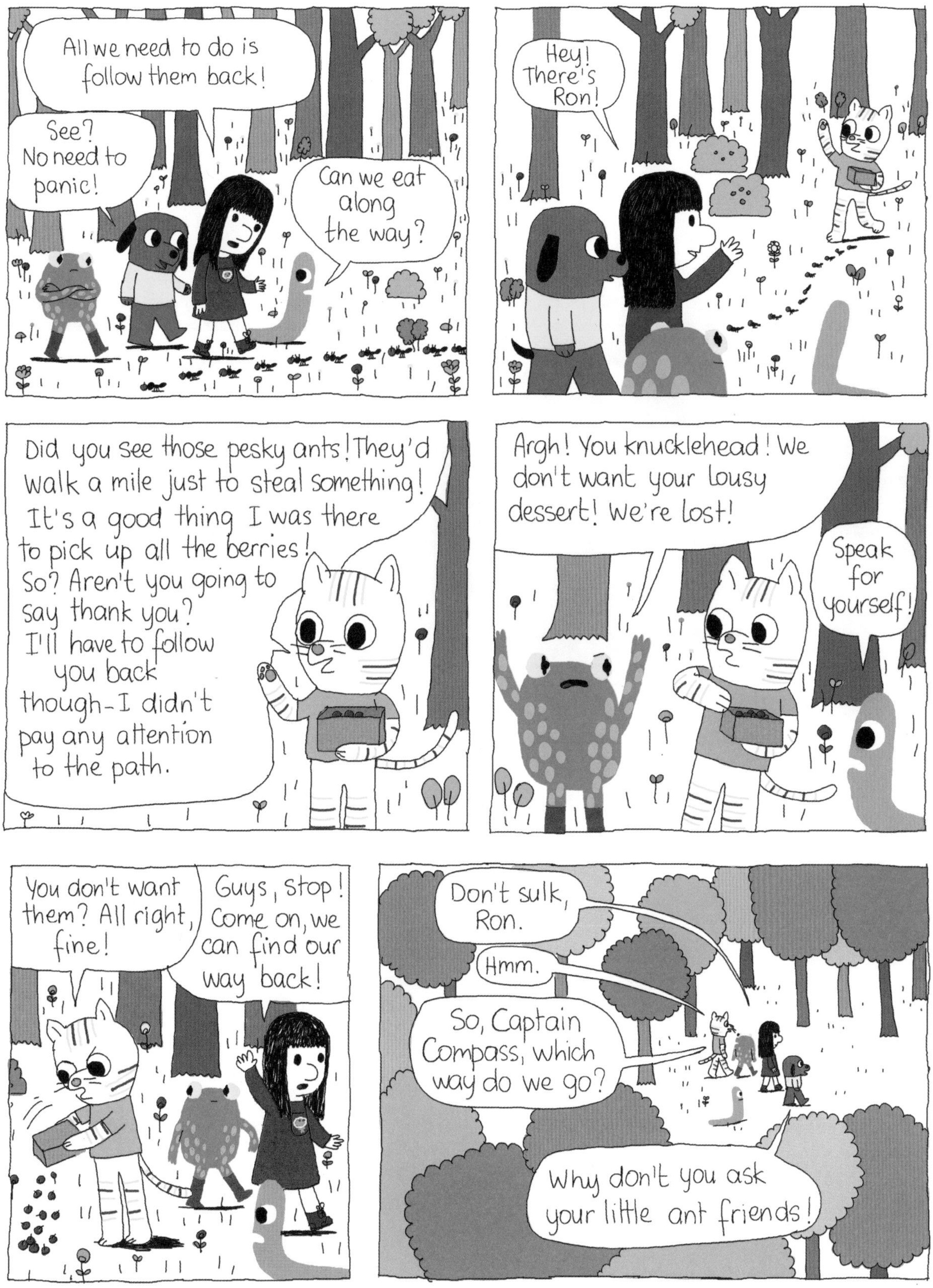
All we need to do is follow them back!
See? No need to panic!
Can we eat along the way?
Hey! There's Ron!
Did you see those pesky ants! They'd walk a mile just to steal something! It's a good thing I was there to pick up all the berries! So? Aren't you going to say thank you? I'll have to follow you back though - I didn't pay any attention to the path.
Argh! You knucklehead! We don't want your lousy dessert! We're lost!
Speak for yourself!
You don't want them? All right, fine!
Guys, stop! Come on, we can find our way back!
Don't sulk, Ron.
Hmm.
So, Captain Compass, which way do we go?
Why don't you ask your little ant friends!

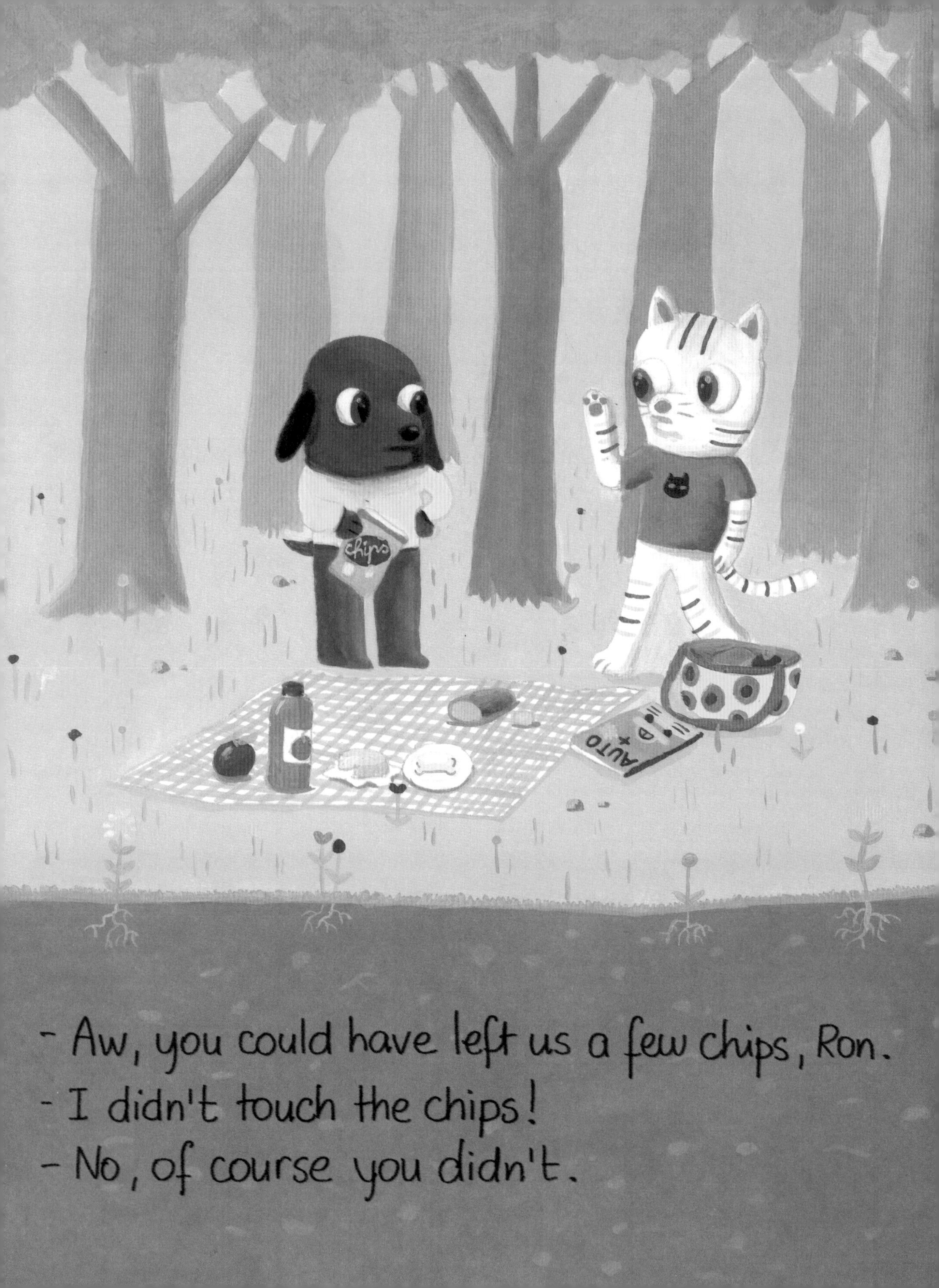
chips
AUTO

- Aw, you could have left us a few chips, Ron.
- I didn't touch the chips!
- No, of course you didn't.

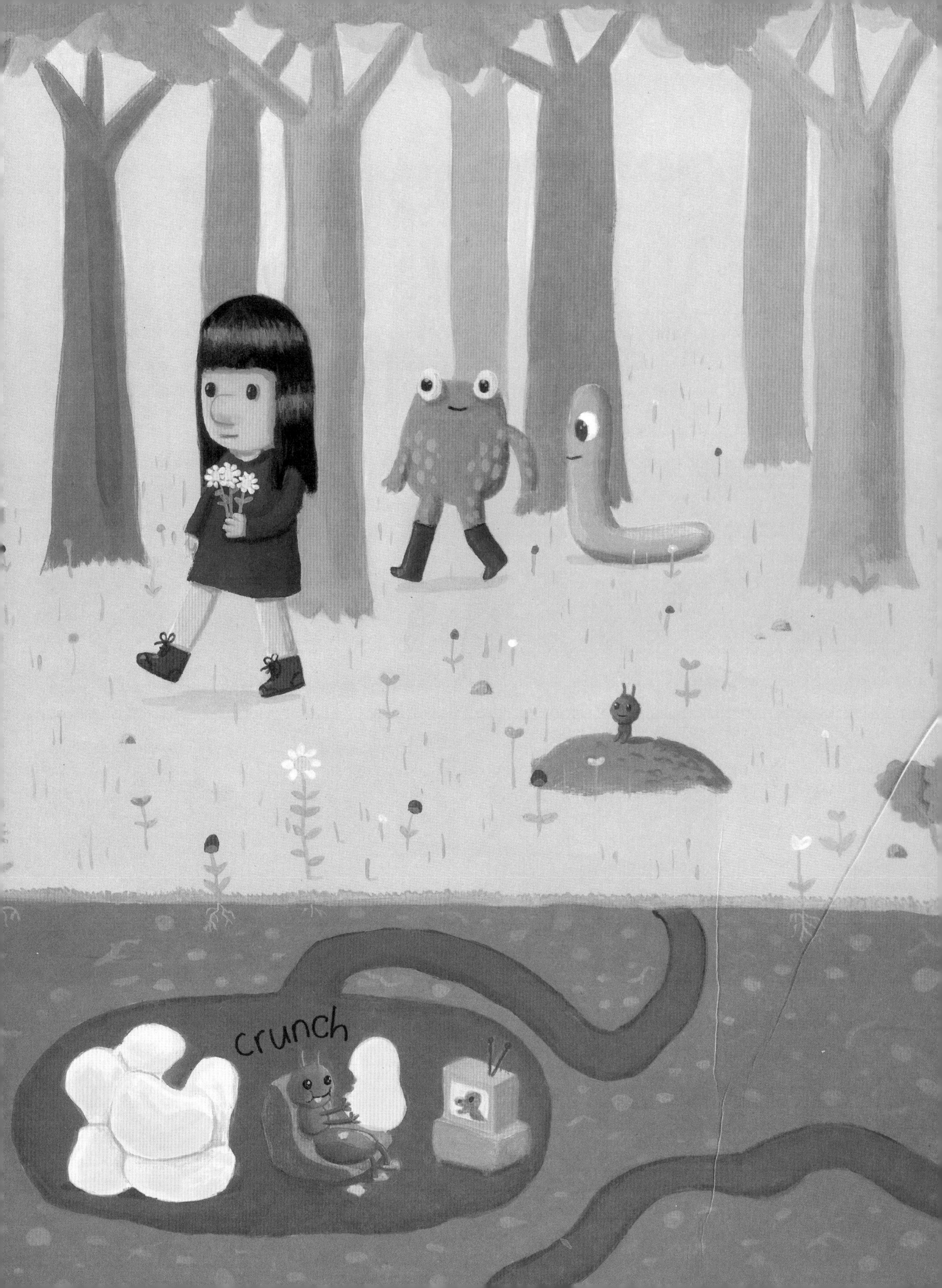
crunch

Maestro Bubu

Still life

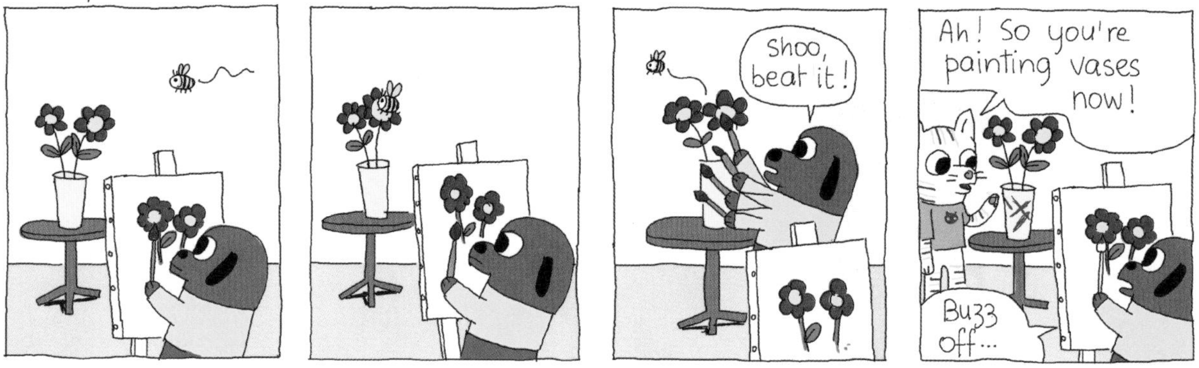
Shoo, beat it!
Ah! So you're painting vases now!
Buzz off...

Abstract art

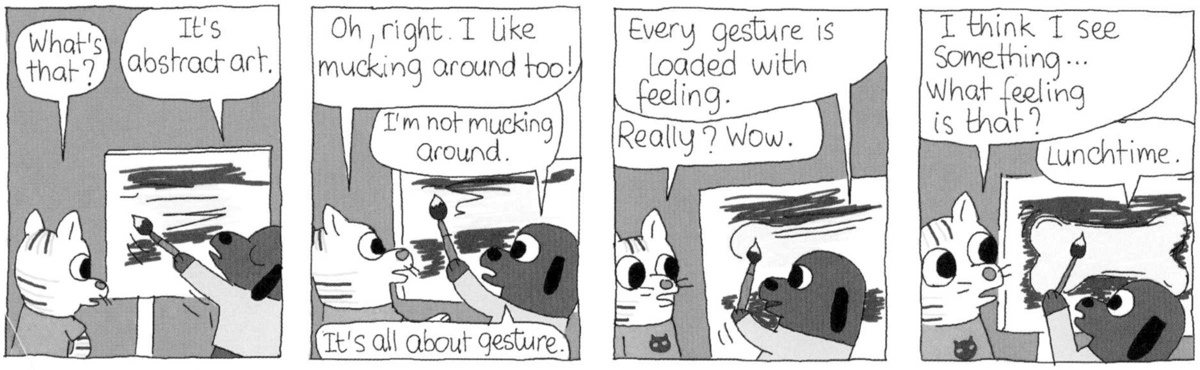
What's that?
It's abstract art.
Oh, right. I like mucking around too!
I'm not mucking around.
It's all about gesture.
Every gesture is loaded with feeling.
Really? Wow.
I think I see something... What feeling is that?
Lunchtime.

The portrait

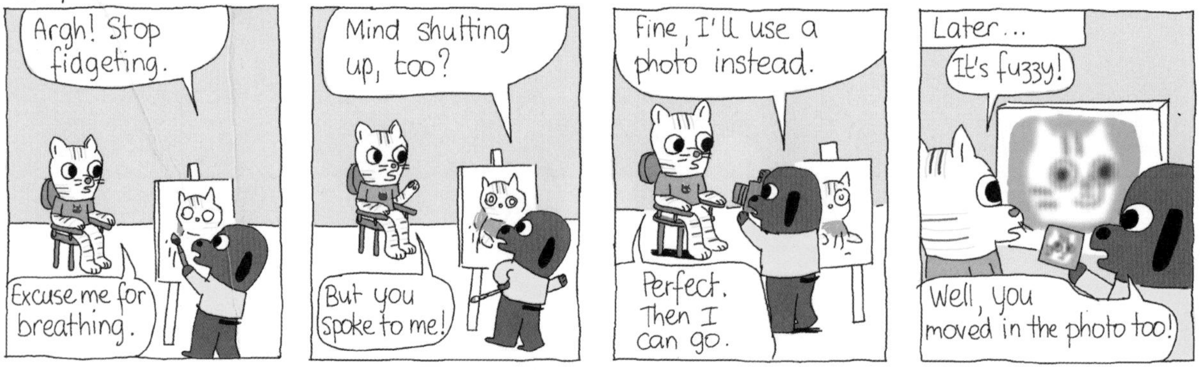
Argh! Stop fidgeting.
Excuse me for breathing.
Mind shutting up, too?
But you spoke to me!
Fine, I'll use a photo instead.
Perfect. Then I can go.
Later...
It's fuzzy!
Well, you moved in the photo too!

Cubism

I'm going to make cubist art today!
I'll start with a cube, that'll be easy!
Hmpf... The corners are kind of tricky.
Messed up, huh?
Not at all. This is spherism.

The landscape

Sunset

The masterpiece

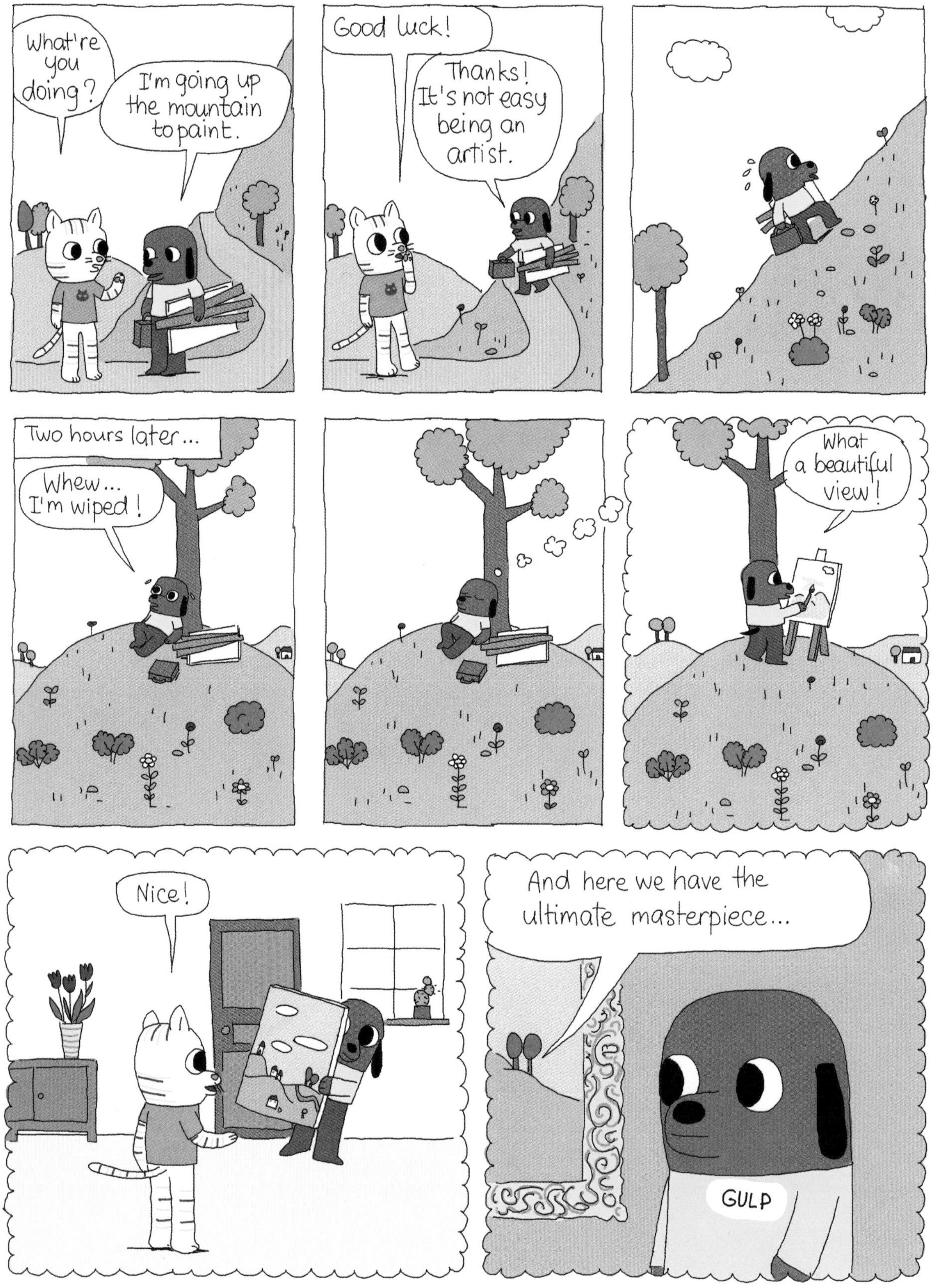
What're you doing?
I'm going up the mountain to paint.
Good luck!
Thanks! It's not easy being an artist.
Two hours later...
Whew... I'm wiped!
What a beautiful view!
Nice!
And here we have the ultimate masterpiece...
GULP

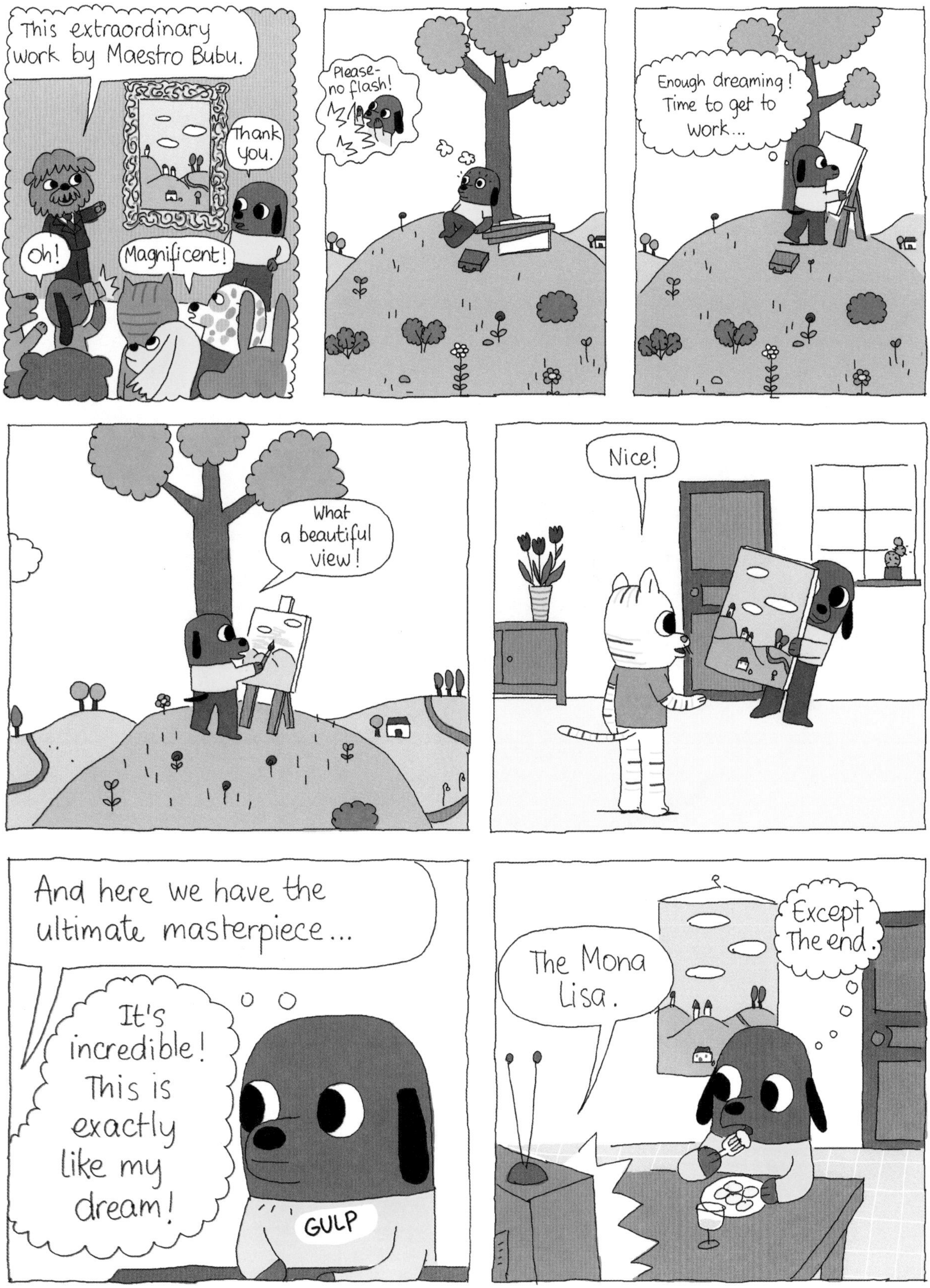
This extraordinary work by Maestro Bubu.
Thank you.
Oh!
Magnificent!
Please- no flash!
Enough dreaming! Time to get to work...
What a beautiful view!
Nice!
And here we have the ultimate masterpiece...
It's incredible! This is exactly like my dream!
GULP
The Mona Lisa.
Except The end.

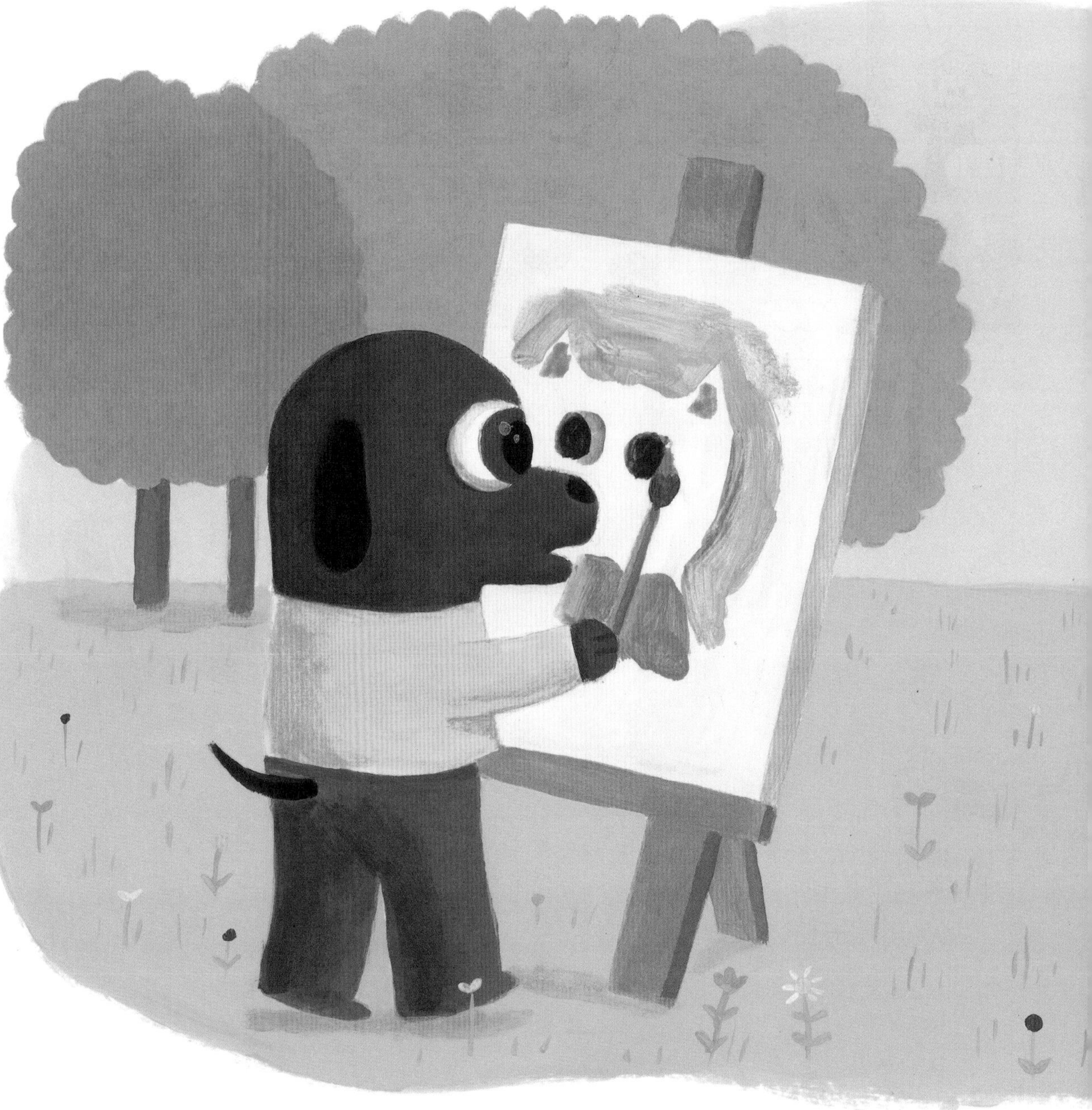

– Whatever you do, don't move!

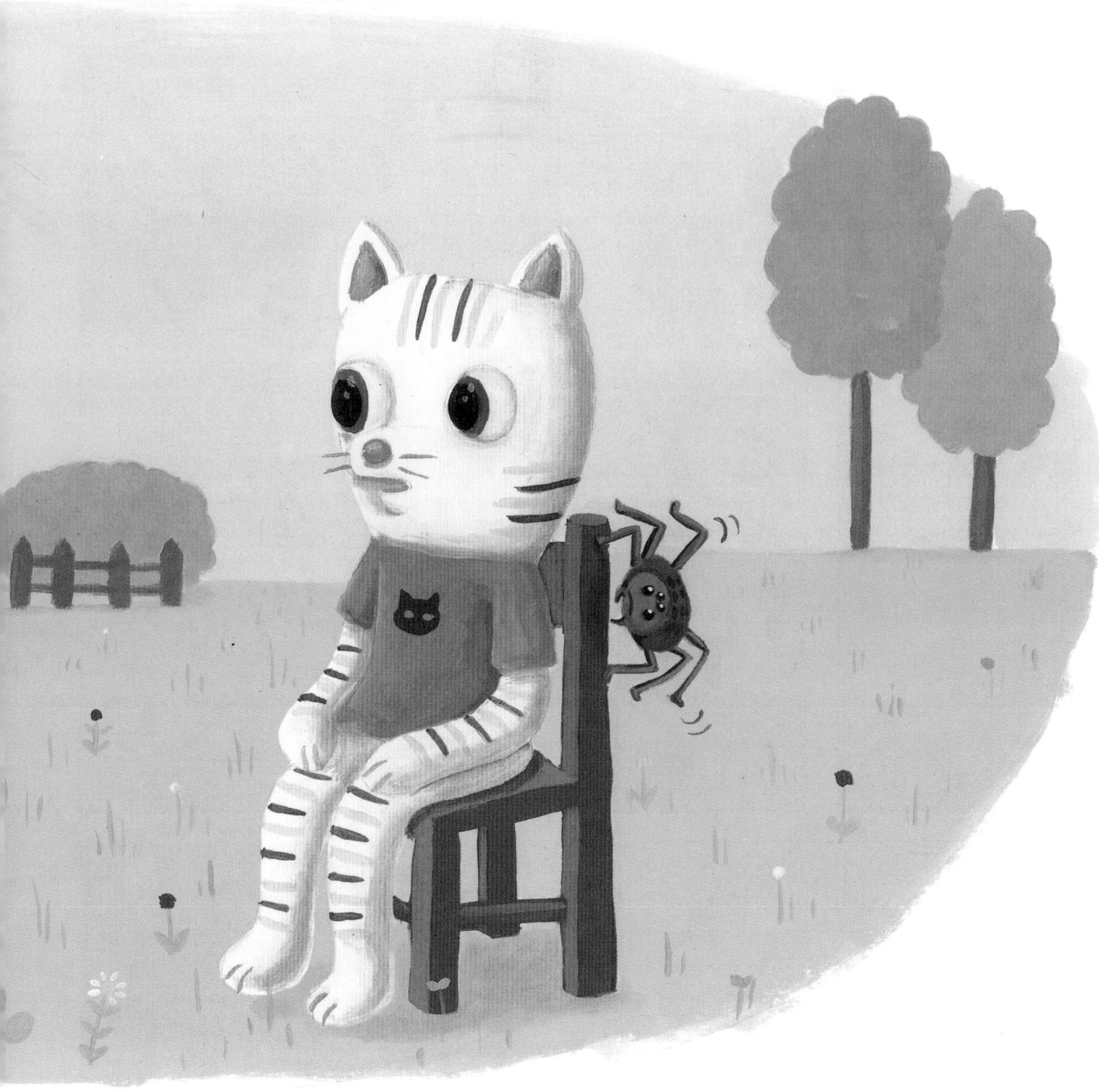

- Yeah, yeah, I know!

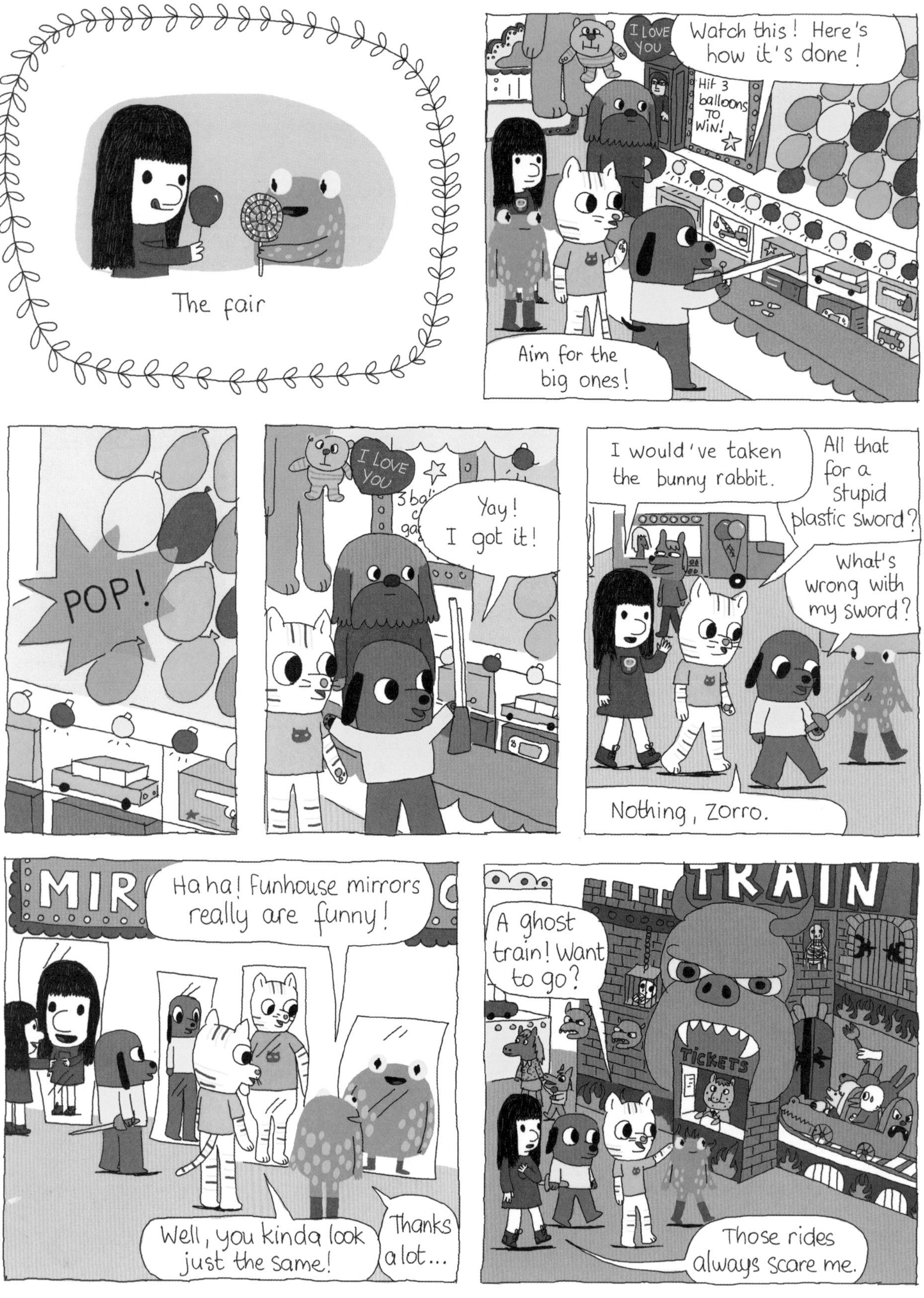
The fair
I LOVE YOU
Watch this! Here's how it's done!
Hit 3 balloons TO WIN!
Aim for the big ones!
POP!
I LOVE YOU
Yay! I got it!
I would've taken the bunny rabbit.
All that for a stupid plastic sword?
What's wrong with my sword?
Nothing, Zorro.
MIR
Ha ha! Funhouse mirrors really are funny!
Well, you kinda look just the same!
Thanks a lot...
TRAIN
A ghost train! Want to go?
TICKETS
Those rides always scare me.

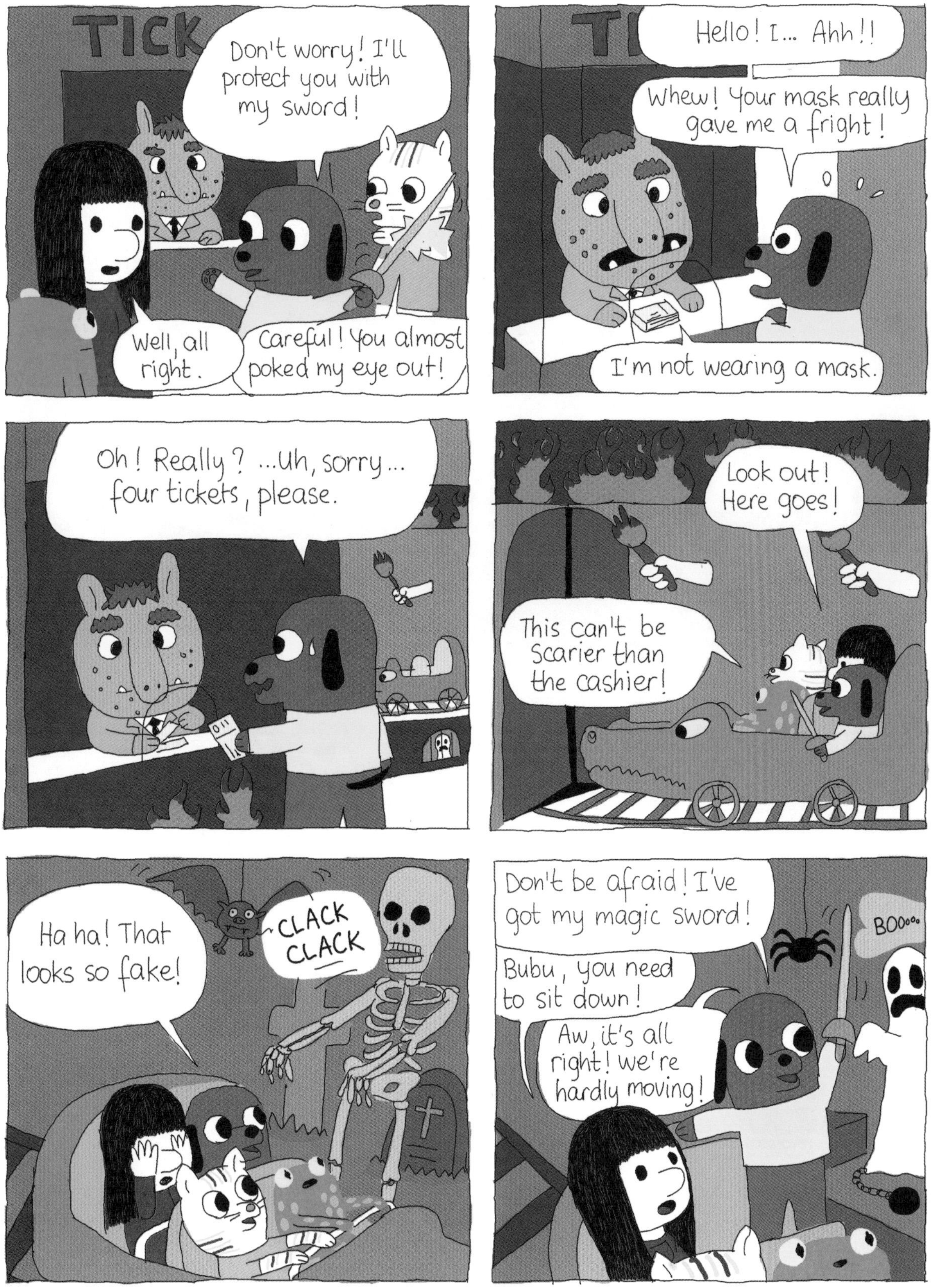
TICK
Don't worry! I'll protect you with my sword!
Well, all right.
Careful! You almost poked my eye out!
TI
Hello! I... Ahh!!
Whew! Your mask really gave me a fright!
I'm not wearing a mask.
Oh! Really? ...uh, sorry... four tickets, please.
Look out! Here goes!
This can't be scarier than the cashier!
Ha ha! That looks so fake!
CLACK CLACK
Don't be afraid! I've got my magic sword!
BOOooo
Bubu, you need to sit down!
Aw, it's all right! We're hardly moving!

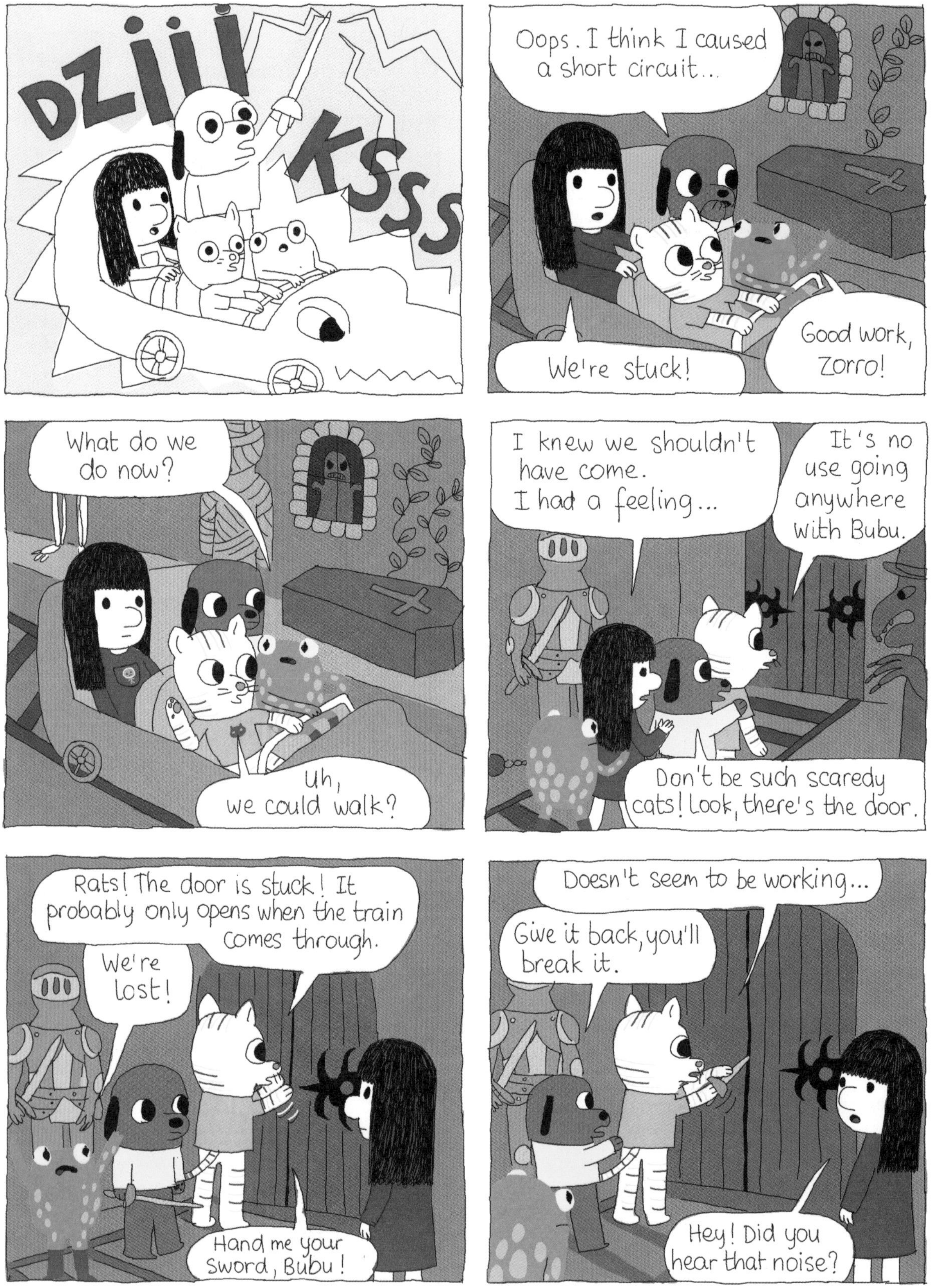
DZIIII KSSS
Oops. I think I caused a short circuit...
We're stuck!
Good work, Zorro!
What do we do now?
Uh, we could walk?
I knew we shouldn't have come. I had a feeling...
It's no use going anywhere with Bubu.
Don't be such scaredy cats! Look, there's the door.
Rats! The door is stuck! It probably only opens when the train comes through.
We're lost!
Hand me your sword, Bubu!
Doesn't seem to be working...
Give it back, you'll break it.
Hey! Did you hear that noise?

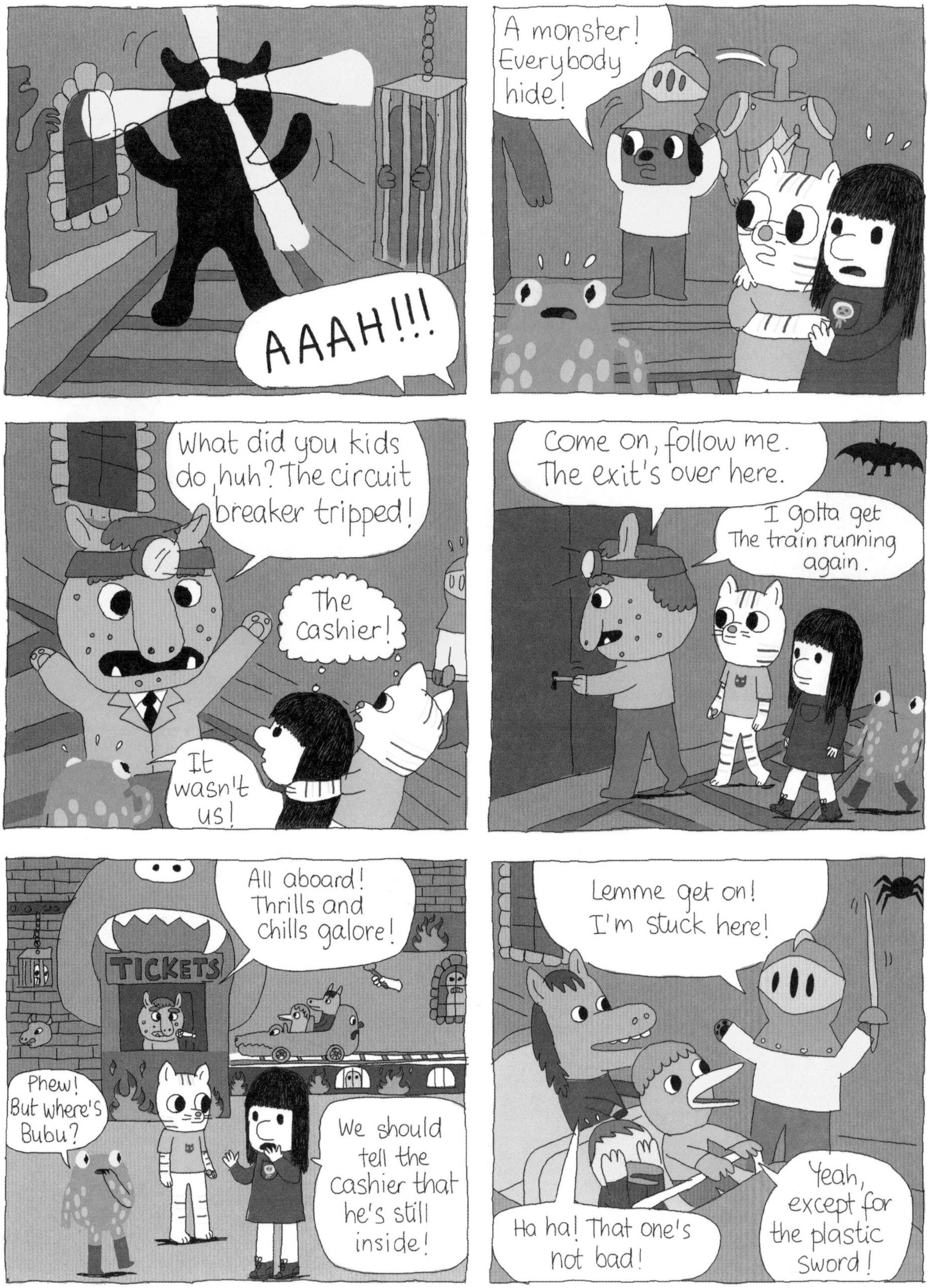
AAAH!!!
A monster! Everybody hide!
What did you kids do, huh? The circuit breaker tripped!
The cashier!
It wasn't us!
Come on, follow me. The exit's over here.
I gotta get the train running again.
All aboard! Thrills and chills galore!
TICKETS
Phew! But where's Bubu?
We should tell the cashier that he's still inside!
Lemme get on! I'm stuck here!
Ha ha! That one's not bad!
Yeah, except for the plastic sword!

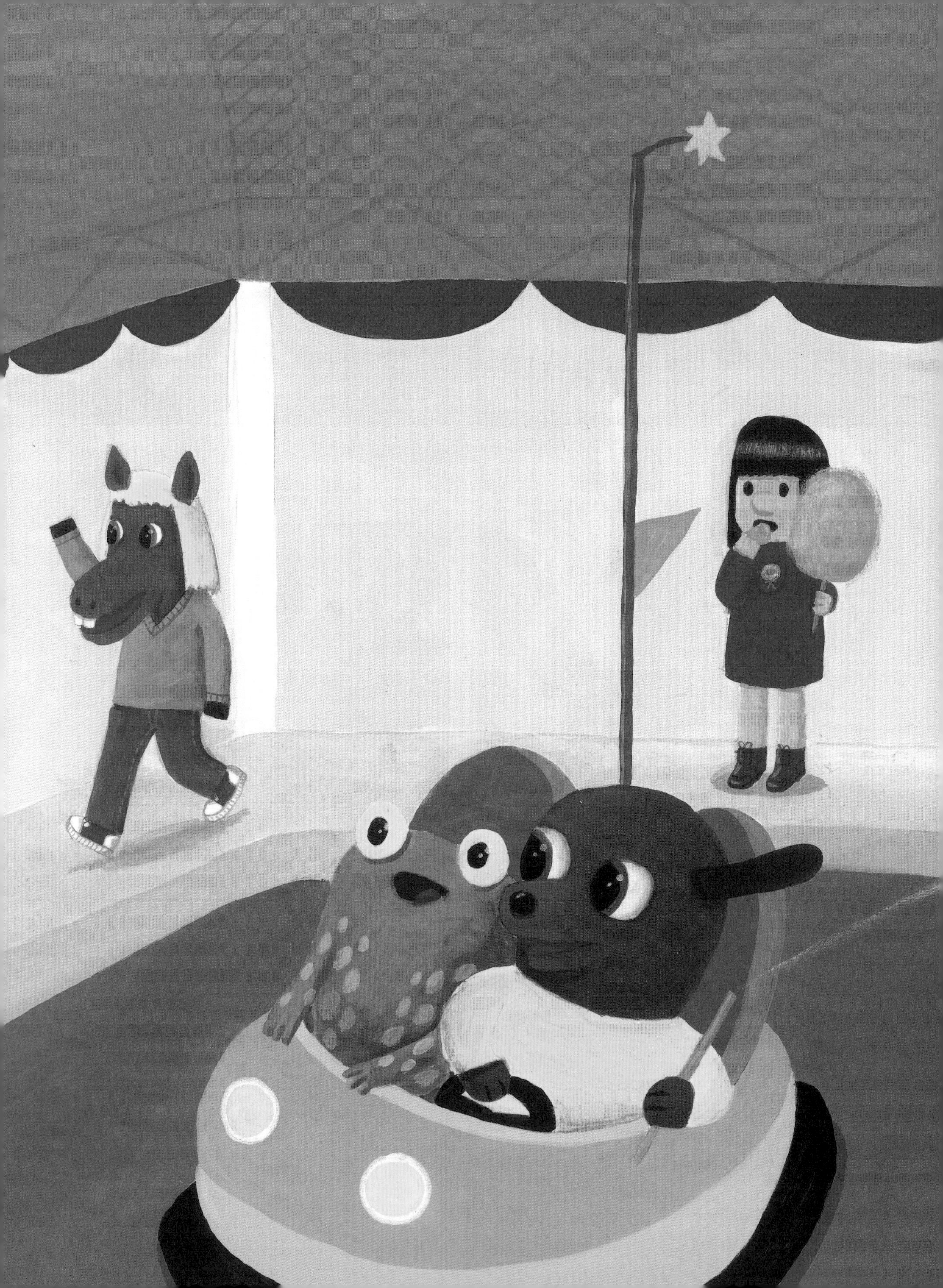

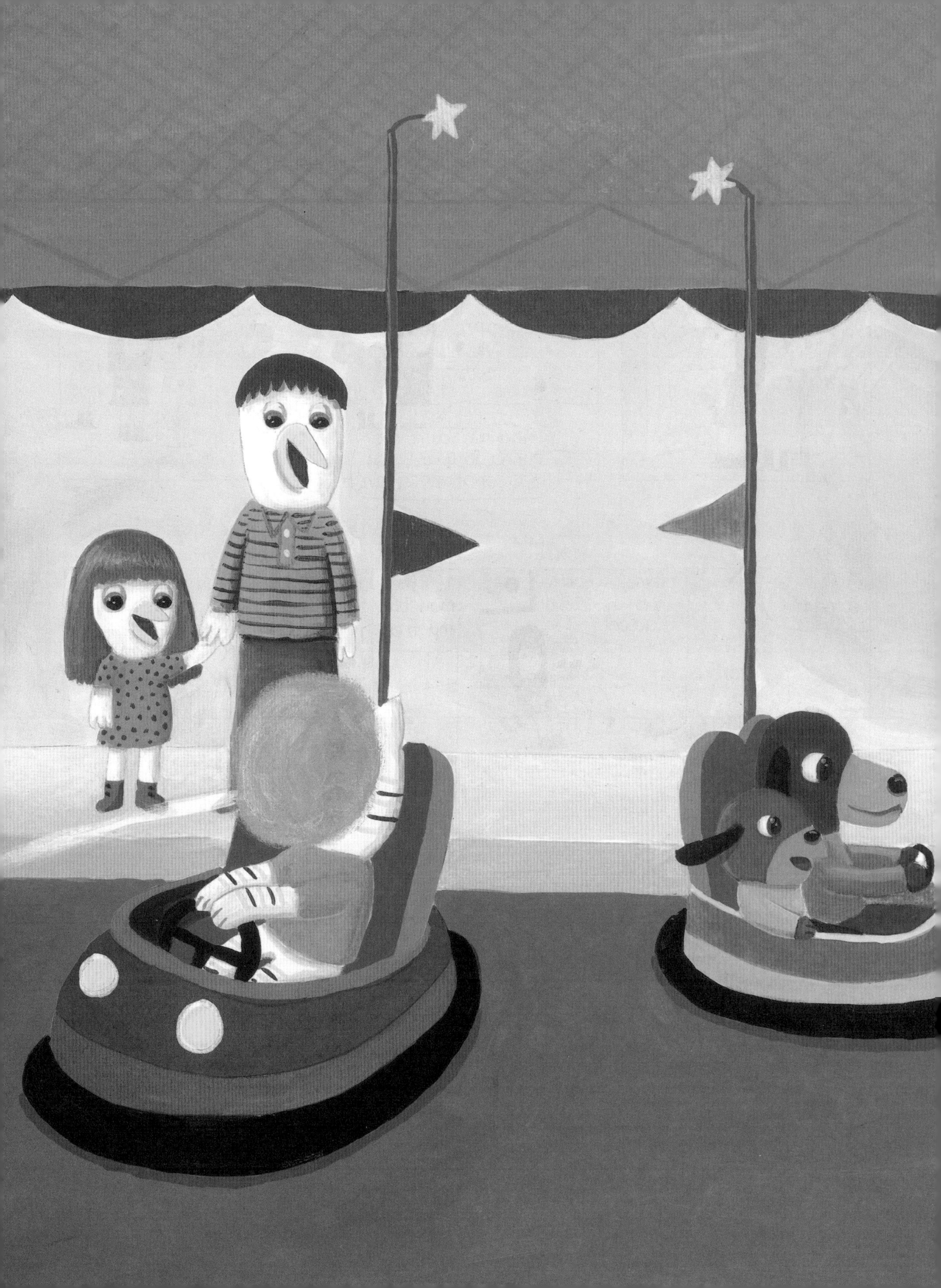

Rainy day games

Guess who 1

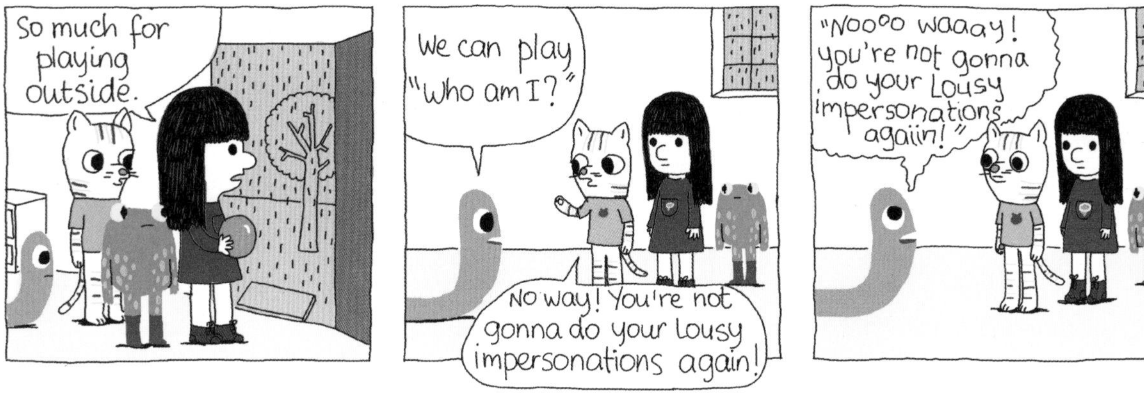
So much for playing outside.
We can play "Who am I?"
No way! You're not gonna do your lousy impersonations again!
"Noo°o waaay! You're not gonna do your lousy impersonations agaiin!"

Guess who 2

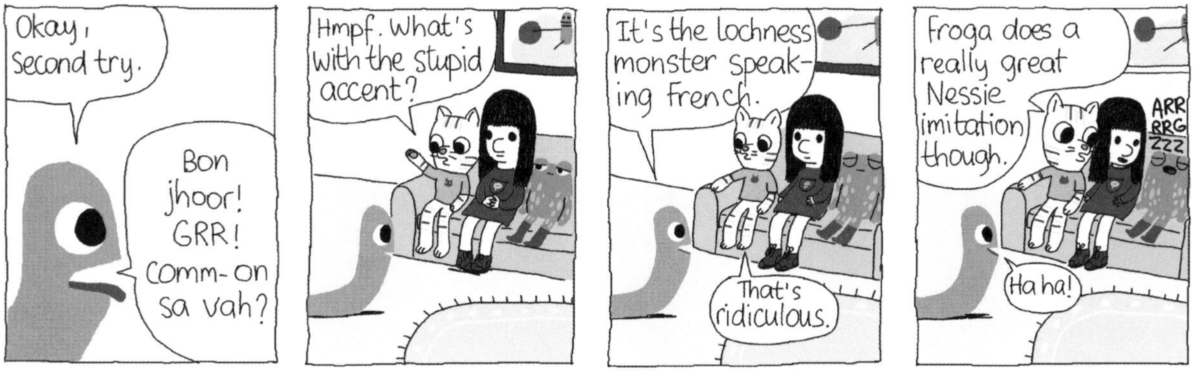
Okay, second try.
Bon jhoor! GRR! Comm-on sa vah?
Hmpf. What's with the stupid accent?
It's the lochness monster speak-ing French.
That's ridiculous.
Froga does a really great Nessie imitation though.
ARR RRG ZZZ
Ha ha!

Guess who 3

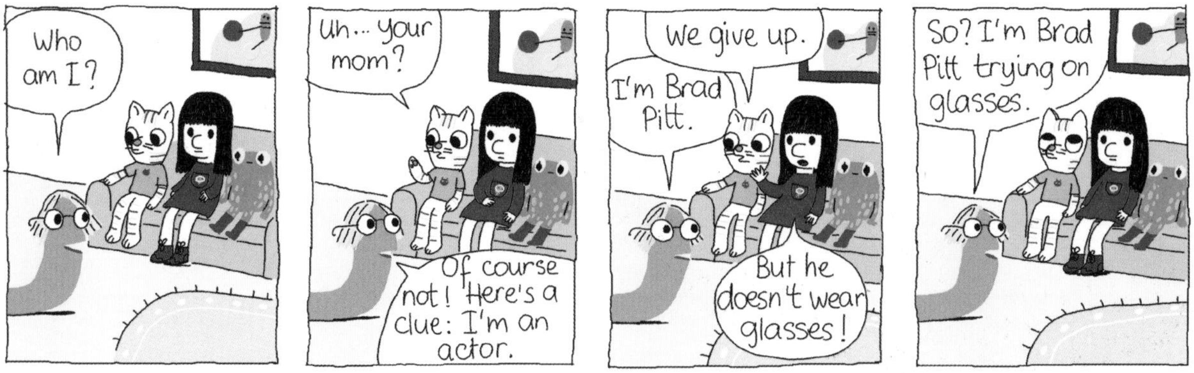
Who am I?
Uh... your mom?
Of course not! Here's a clue: I'm an actor.
We give up.
I'm Brad Pitt.
But he doesn't wear glasses!
So? I'm Brad Pitt trying on glasses.

Nailed

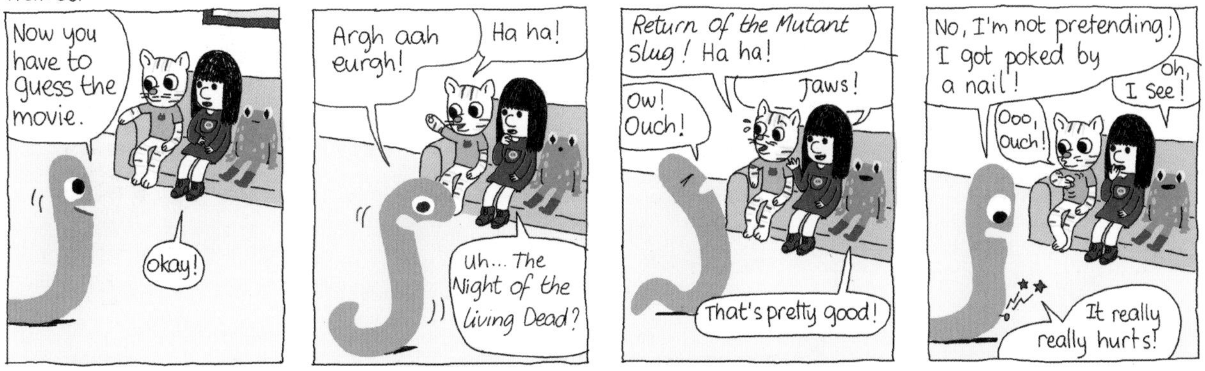

Now you have to guess the movie.
Okay!
Argh aah eurgh!
Ha ha!
Uh... The Night of the Living Dead?
Return of the Mutant Slug! Ha ha!
Jaws!
Ow! Ouch!
That's pretty good!
No, I'm not pretending! I got poked by a nail!
Oh, I see!
Ooo, ouch!
It really really hurts!

Nailed 2

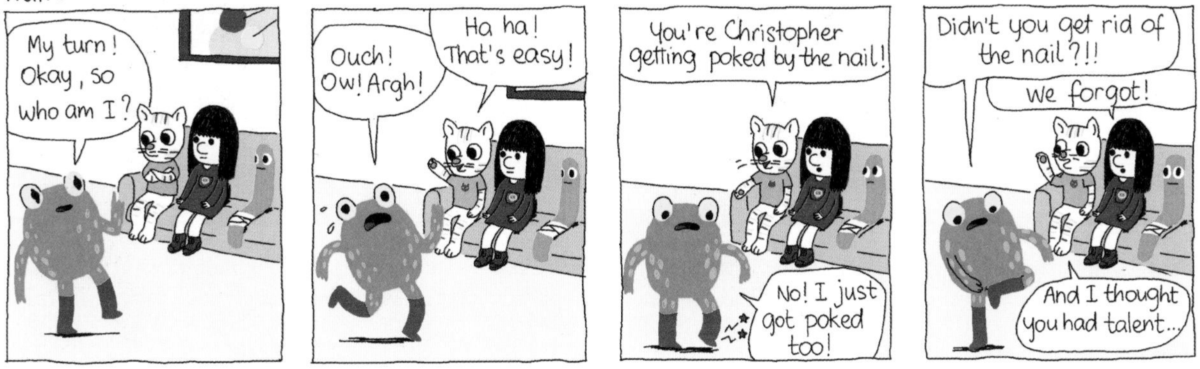

My turn! Okay, so who am I?
Ouch! Ow! Argh!
Ha ha! That's easy!
You're Christopher getting poked by the nail!
No! I just got poked too!
Didn't you get rid of the nail?!!
We forgot!
And I thought you had talent...

The name

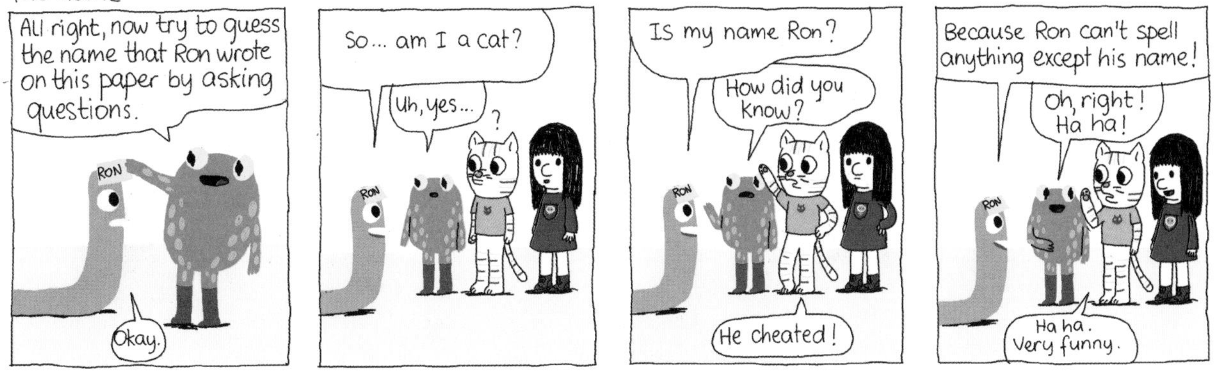

All right, now try to guess the name that Ron wrote on this paper by asking questions.
RON
Okay.
So... am I a cat?
Uh, yes...
?
Is my name Ron?
How did you know?
He cheated!
Because Ron can't spell anything except his name!
Oh, right! Ha ha!
Ha ha. Very funny.

Who am I?

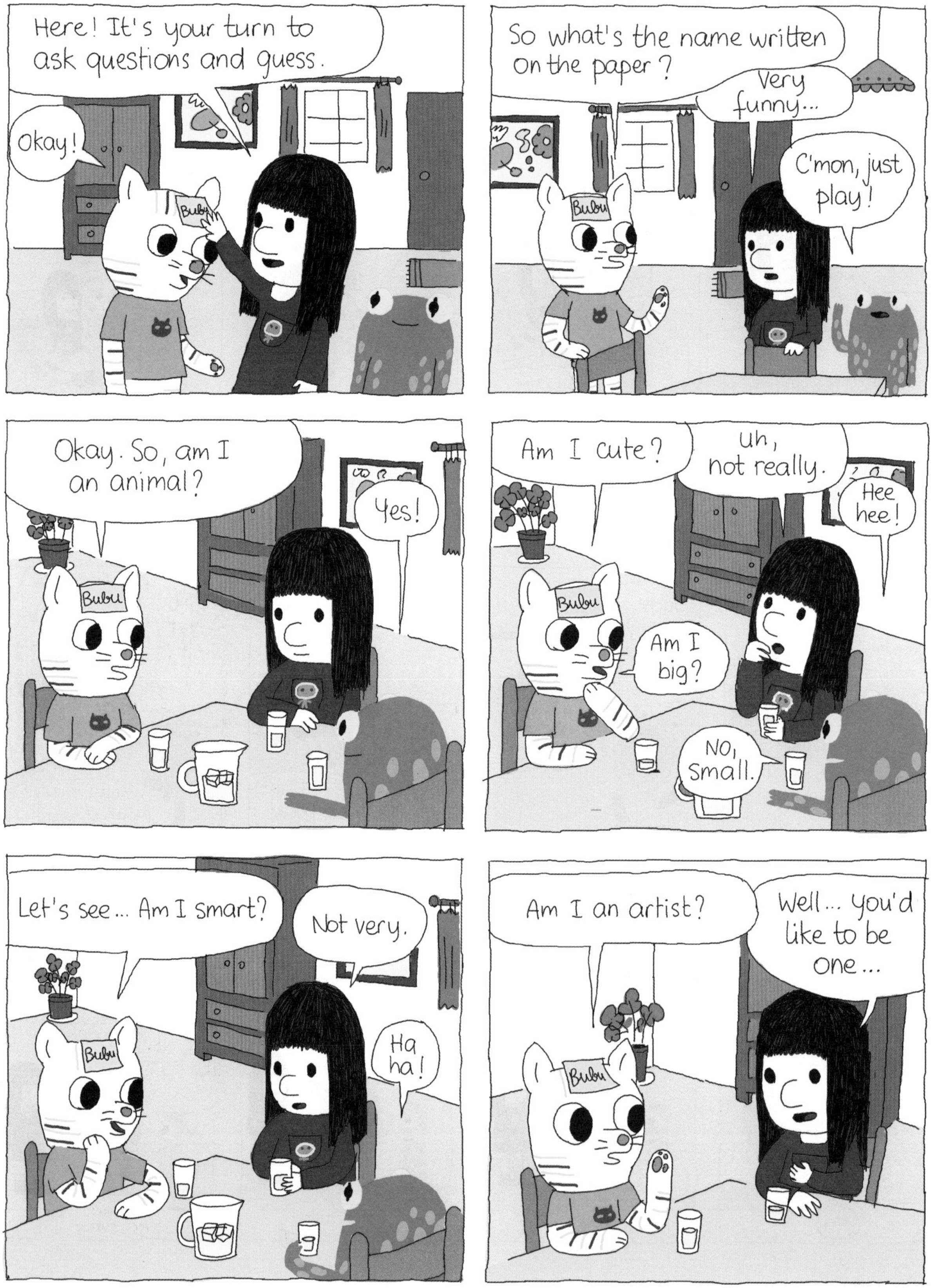

Here! It's your turn to ask questions and guess.
Okay!
Bubu
So what's the name written on the paper?
Very funny...
C'mon, just play!
Bubu
Okay. So, am I an animal?
Yes!
Bubu
Am I cute?
Uh, not really.
Hee hee!
Am I big?
No, small.
Bubu
Let's see... Am I smart?
Not very.
Ha ha!
Bubu
Am I an artist?
Well... you'd like to be one...
Bubu

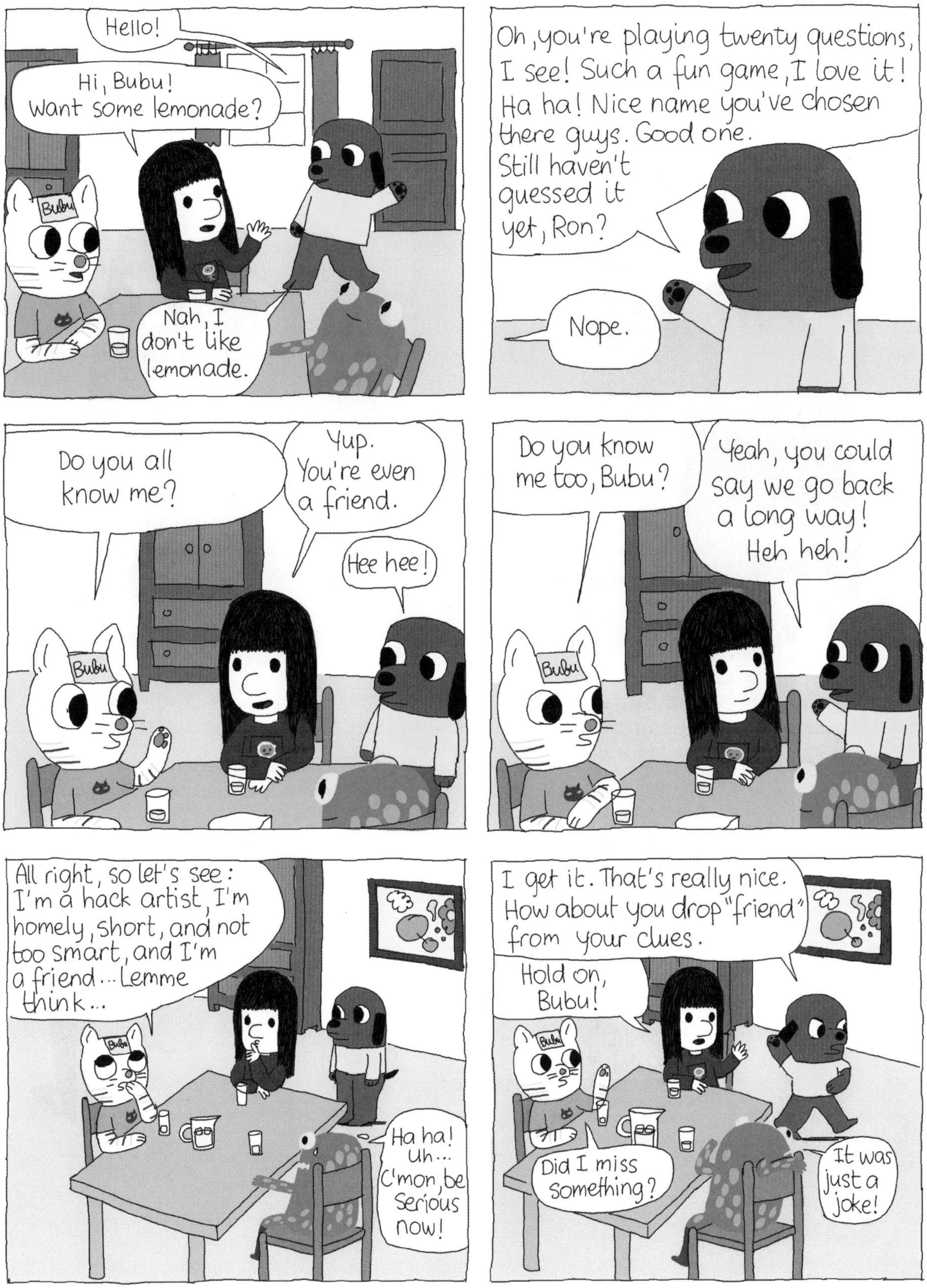

Hello!
Hi, Bubu! Want some lemonade?
Nah, I don't like lemonade.
Bubu
Oh, you're playing twenty questions, I see! Such a fun game, I love it! Ha ha! Nice name you've chosen there guys. Good one.
Still haven't guessed it yet, Ron?
Nope.
Do you all know me?
Yup. You're even a friend.
Hee hee!
Bubu
Do you know me too, Bubu?
Yeah, you could say we go back a long way! Heh heh!
Bubu
All right, so let's see: I'm a hack artist, I'm homely, short, and not too smart, and I'm a friend... Lemme think...
Ha ha! Uh... C'mon, be serious now!
I get it. That's really nice. How about you drop "friend" from your clues.
Hold on, Bubu!
Did I miss something?
It was just a joke!

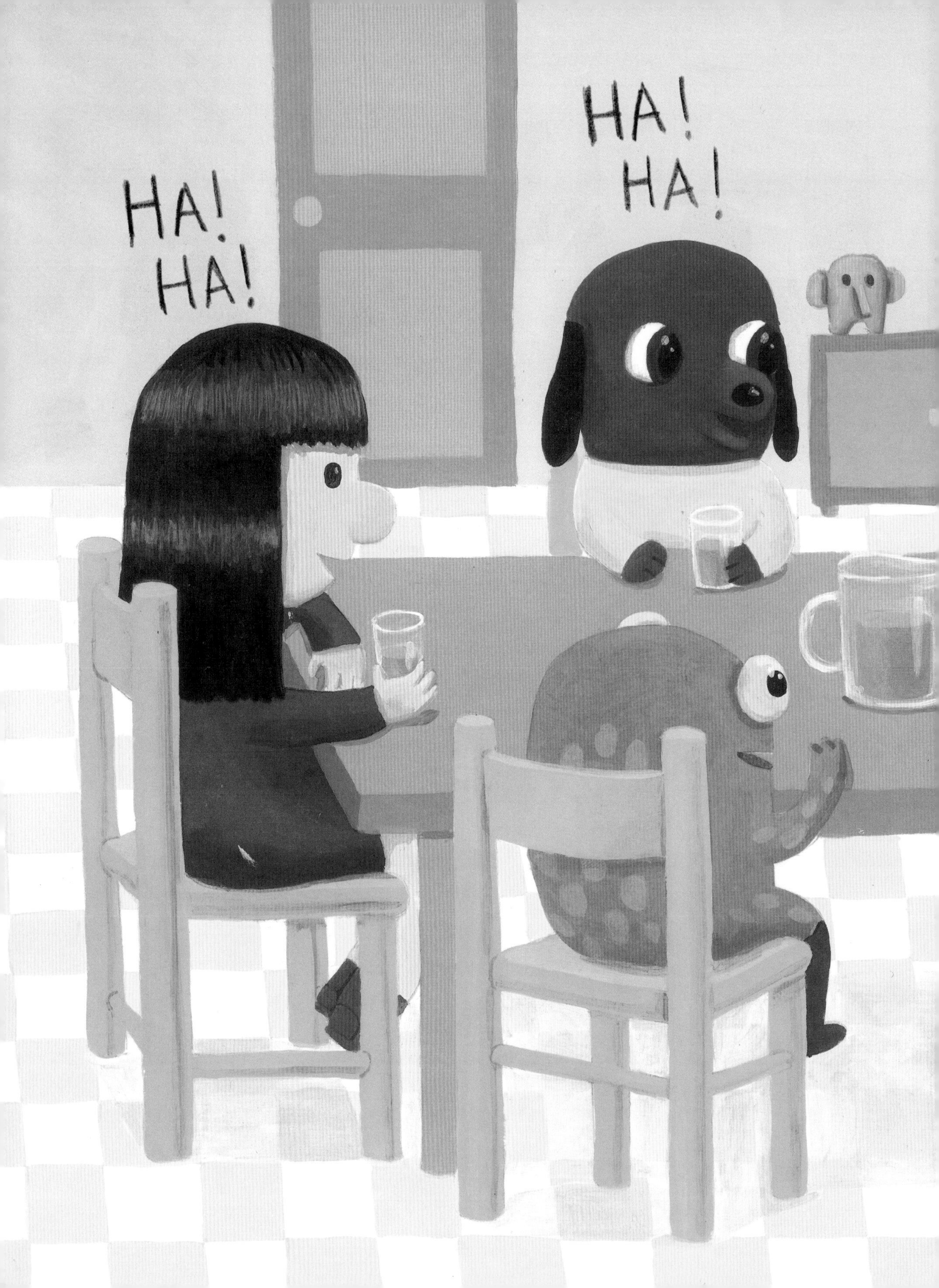
HA! HA!
HA! HA!

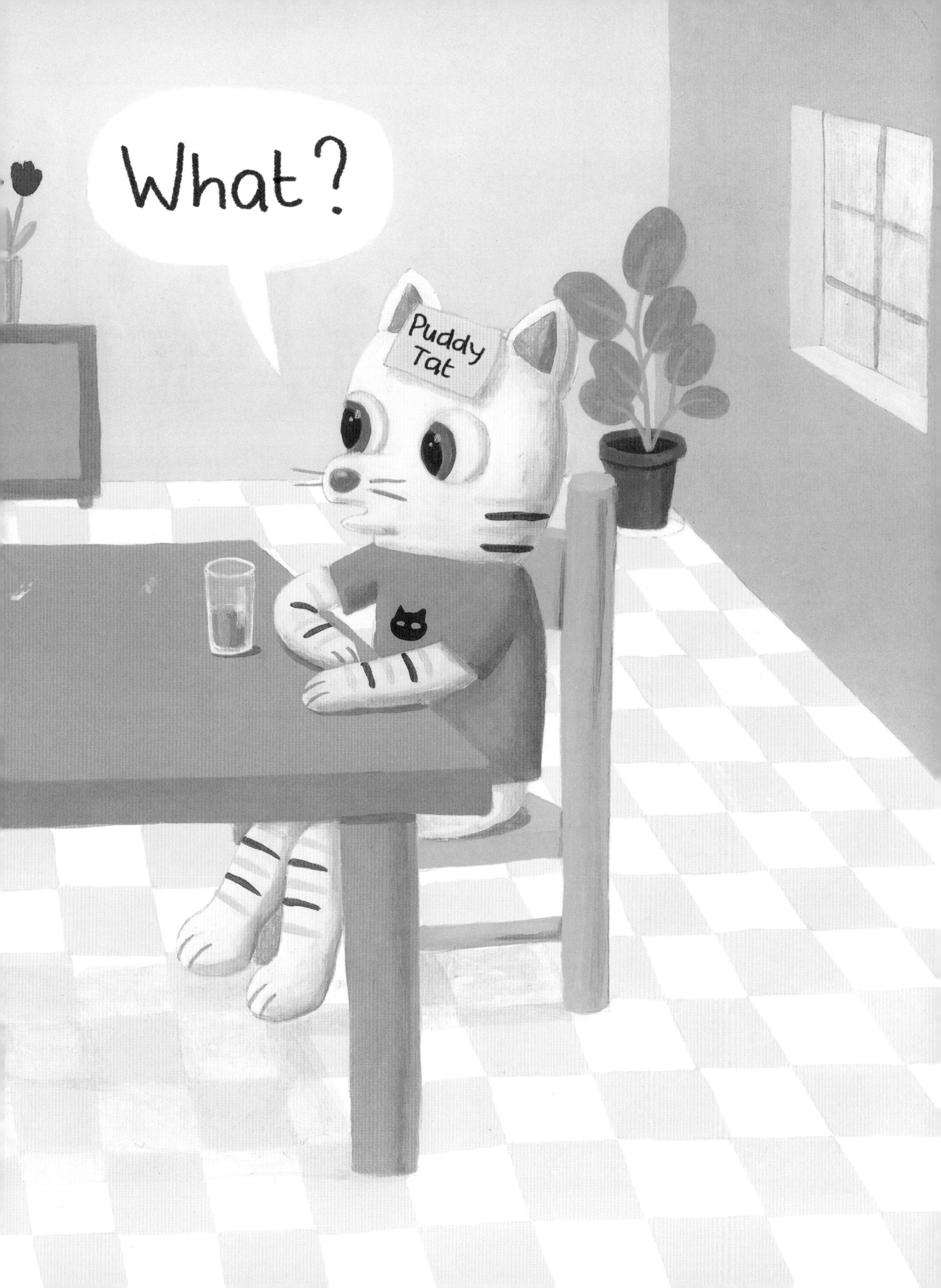
What?
Puddy Tat

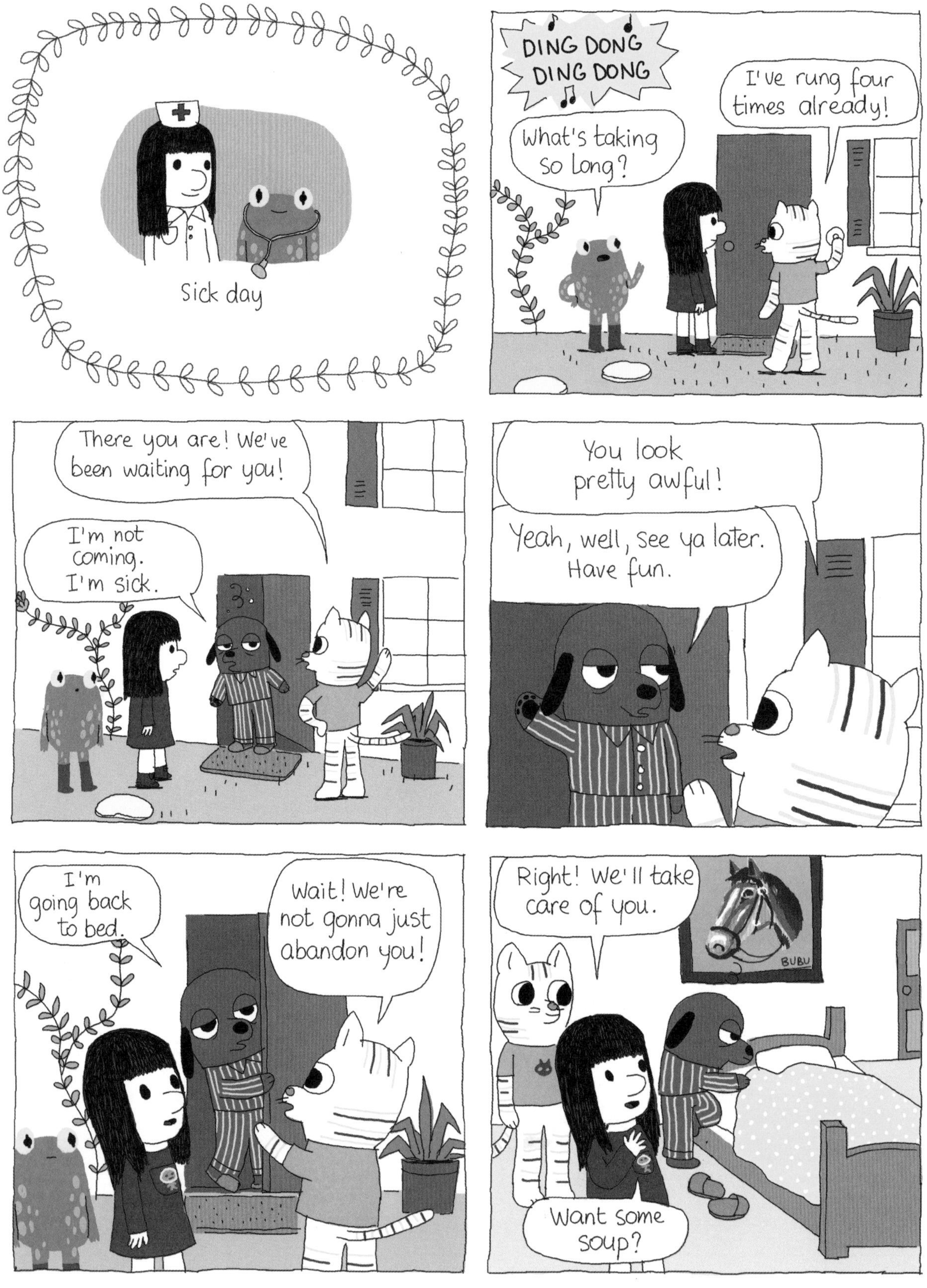
Sick day
DING DONG DING DONG
What's taking so long?
I've rung four times already!
There you are! We've been waiting for you!
I'm not coming. I'm sick.
You look pretty awful!
Yeah, well, see ya later. Have fun.
I'm going back to bed.
Wait! We're not gonna just abandon you!
Right! We'll take care of you.
BUBU
Want some soup?

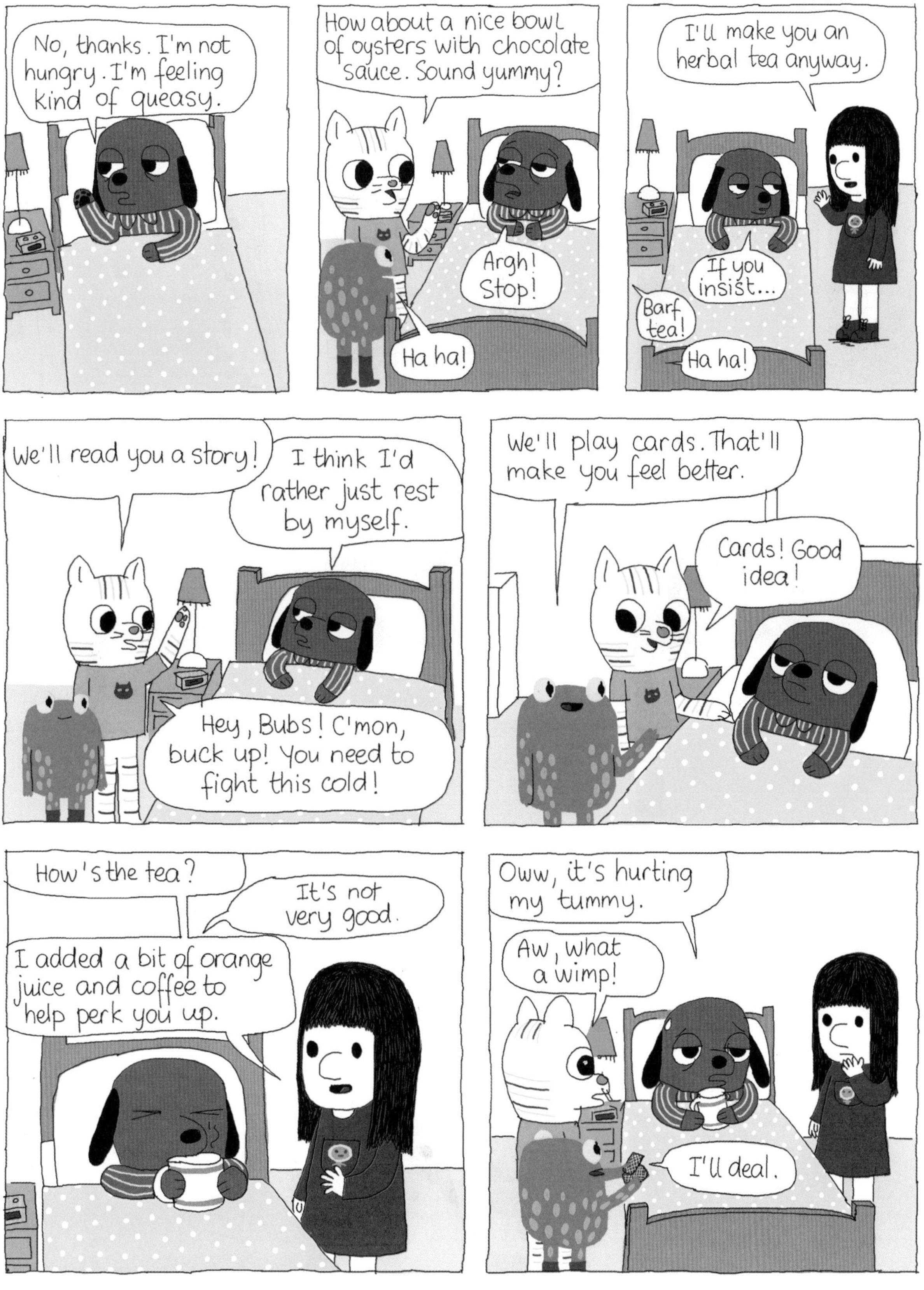
No, thanks. I'm not hungry. I'm feeling kind of queasy.
How about a nice bowl of oysters with chocolate sauce. Sound yummy?
Argh! Stop!
Ha ha!
I'll make you an herbal tea anyway.
If you insist...
Barf tea!
Ha ha!
We'll read you a story!
I think I'd rather just rest by myself.
Hey, Bubs! C'mon, buck up! You need to fight this cold!
We'll play cards. That'll make you feel better.
Cards! Good idea!
How's the tea?
It's not very good.
I added a bit of orange juice and coffee to help perk you up.
Oww, it's hurting my tummy.
Aw, what a wimp!
I'll deal.

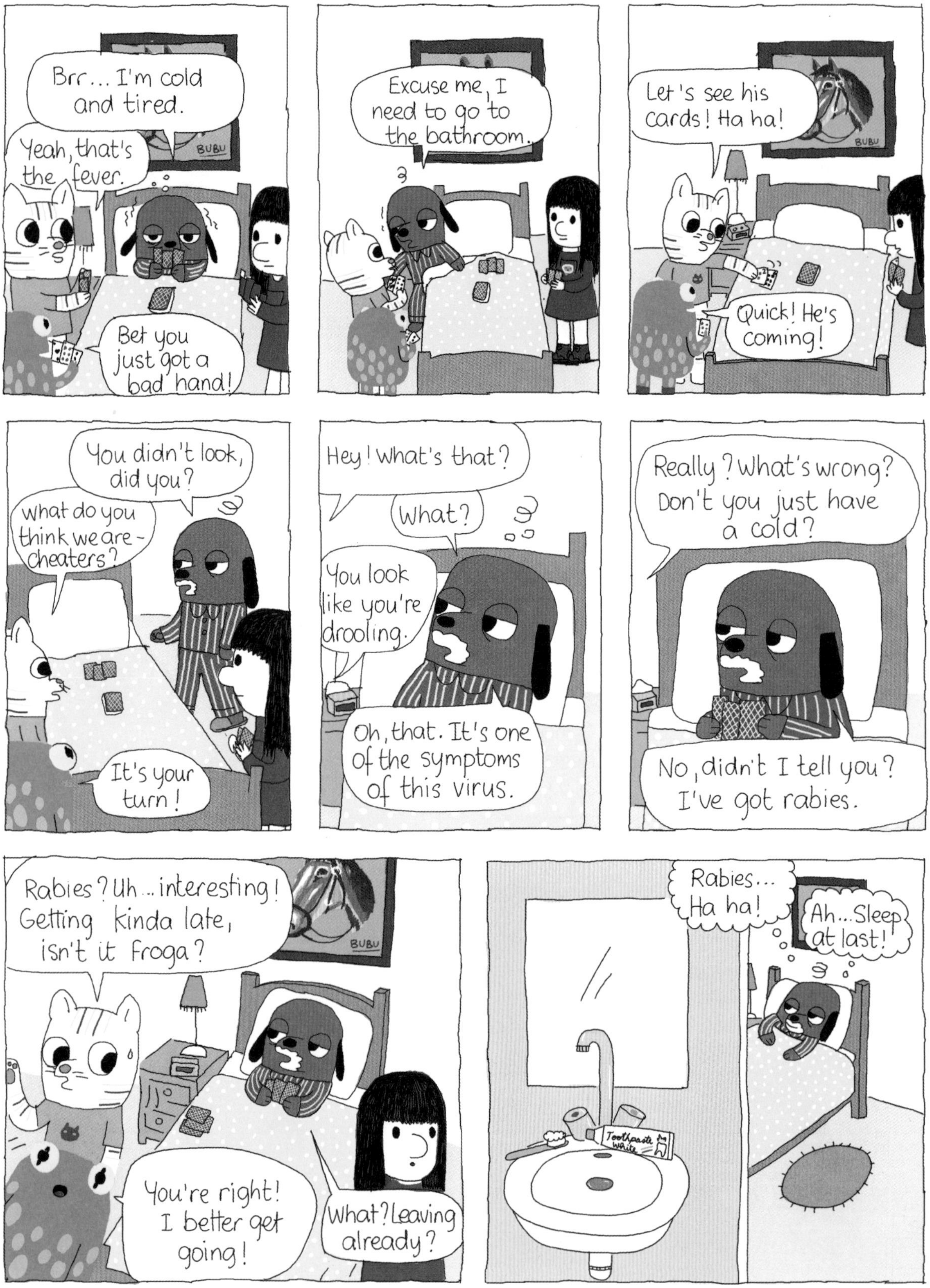
Brr... I'm cold and tired.
Yeah, that's the fever.
Bet you just got a bad hand!
Excuse me, I need to go to the bathroom.
Let's see his cards! Ha ha!
Quick! He's coming!
You didn't look, did you?
What do you think we are - cheaters?
It's your turn!
Hey! What's that?
What?
You look like you're drooling.
Oh, that. It's one of the symptoms of this virus.
Really? What's wrong? Don't you just have a cold?
No, didn't I tell you? I've got rabies.
Rabies? Uh... interesting! Getting kinda late, isn't it Froga?
You're right! I better get going!
What? Leaving already?
Rabies... Ha ha!
Ah... Sleep at last!
Toothpaste White
BUBU

Hello, Bubu? We're going to keep you company by phone so we don't get sick. Ron has lots of jokes to tell you. Are we great friends or what?
All right, so a guy is walking down the street with bananas in his ears when suddenly...

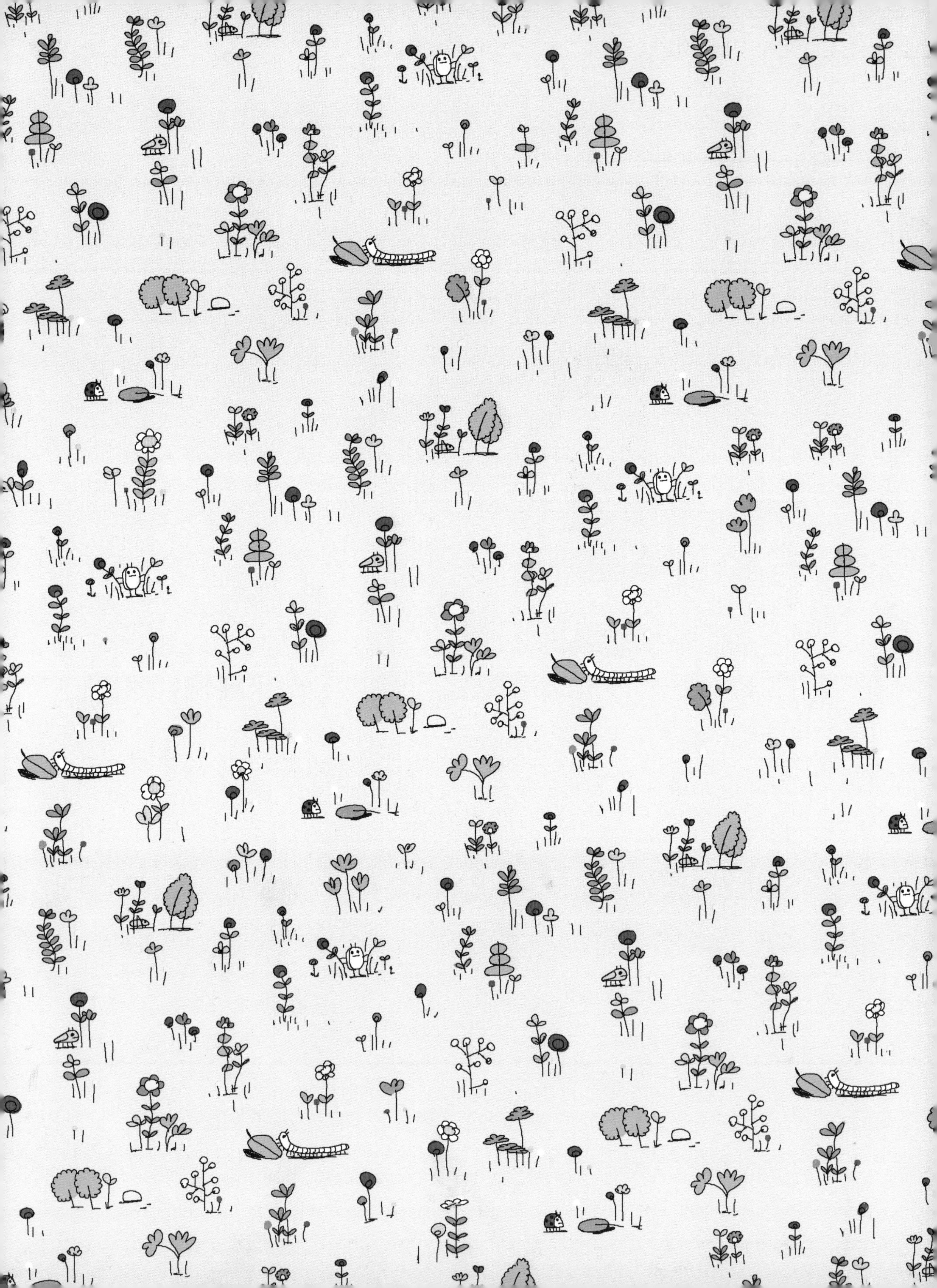